"You don't have t

"I don't need help." She panicked as she imagined him being at the house with her every day, watching her.

As he walked away, he said over his shoulder, "I hope one day you stop seeing me as the enemy and let me be your friend."

"I can't," she said, tears burning her eyes. He was a minister. "I can't be your friend, Rory."

"Or you can't let *me* be your friend?" Before she could answer, he turned back. "I came here today because I saw someone in need. Not as a minister but as a person."

And then he was gone.

Vanessa wanted to run after him. But she had to be strong and fight the temptation. She'd taken care of herself for a long time now. Why should she believe a sweet-talking preacher who made her feel safe?

Her confusing thoughts about Rory had to stop. Because growing close to him would be a bad idea.

So why did she want to believe him?

With sixty books published and millions in print, **Lenora Worth** writes award-winning romance and romantic suspense. Three of her books finaled in the ACFW Carol Awards, and her Love Inspired Suspense novel *Body of Evidence* became a *New York Times* bestseller. Her novella in *Mistletoe Kisses* made her a *USA TODAY* bestselling author. Lenora goes on adventures with her retired husband, Don, and enjoys reading, baking and shopping… especially shoe shopping.

Visit the Author Profile page at Harlequin.com for more titles.

Lakeside
Sweetheart

Lenora Worth

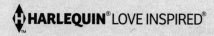

Recycling programs
for this product may
not exist in your area.

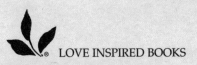

LOVE INSPIRED BOOKS

ISBN-13: 978-0-373-71959-4

Lakeside Sweetheart

www.Harlequin.com

Printed in U.S.A.

Jesus said to her, Everyone who drinks of this water will be thirsty again, but those who drink of the water that I will give them will never be thirsty. The water that I will give will become in them a spring of water gushing up to eternal life.
—*John* 4:13–14

To my cousin Nancy Anderson.
So glad you are back in our lives!

Chapter One

He always noticed new faces at church.

As minister of the Millbrook Lake Church, Rory Sanderson had a bird's-eye view of the entire congregation, including everyone from Mrs. Fanny Fitzpatrick in her fake-fruit covered straw hat to Alec Caldwell's aunt Hattie in her pearls and baby-blue pillbox.

But one person stood out today more than all the others.

Maybe because her discomfort could have shattered the rows of stained glass windows lining each side of the tiny chapel. The doubtful expression made her look a little lost, but her light brown hair shimmered with a luster that reminded him of sea oats at sunrise. He couldn't tell much about her eyes. She wore dark shades.

But he felt pretty sure those hidden eyes were staring straight at him. She must be one of those. Someone had obviously invited her to the service today. And she so did not want to be here.

Rory took that as a challenge. He accepted the woman's distrust with a smile and a prayer. That was his job, after all. To turn that frown upside down. To bring the lost home. To make the backsliders and unbelievers faithful. Especially on such a beautiful spring day. A day full of rebirth and renewal. The best kind of day.

Easter Sunday.

The whole flock, maybe the whole town, had turned out in their Easter finery. And they all had smiles on their faces.

Except for that one, of course. The one in the pretty yellow dress that reminded him of picnics and wildflowers, wearing those dark Wayfarers and that shell-shocked expression. And Rory had to wonder. What had made this woman so reluctant to be here today?

"You could try smiling," Marla Caldwell said into Vanessa Donovan's ear. "It won't break your face."

"I told you I don't do church," Vanessa replied, uneasiness making her fidget. Tugging her turquoise floral wrap over her bare arms, she glanced around. "I only came because you invited me. And because I want some of that good food your mother and Aunt Hattie bribed us with—I mean—promised to us—for Sunday dinner."

"They are not above bribery," Marla said with a grin, her red-gold ponytail bouncing. "But church will do you good, you'll see. It sure can't hurt you."

Marla could afford to tease. She was still a newlywed. Happy and settled and very much in love with a former marine who lived in a big Victorian house not far from Vanessa's smaller Craftsman-style cottage. After a Christmas wedding, Marla and her cute preschooler, Gabby, now lived in that rambling house with handsome Alec Caldwell and his adorable aunt Hattie and two dogs. One big, happy family.

Something Vanessa would never have. But she didn't care about all of that anyway, she reminded herself.

Glad for her friend, Vanessa remembered she didn't

believe in that sort of thing. She was a realist who'd decided long ago that marriage and family weren't for her. Marla teased her about being too pessimistic and cynical, but Vanessa was practical and resolved. Resolved to a life that didn't include a long-term relationship or attending church or bouncing a baby on her lap.

"I'm not quite ready to dive right in," Vanessa said, her eyes on the cute guy up front greeting everyone as if he owned the place. "What's the story with Surfer Dude?"

Marla giggled. "You mean Preacher? His name is Rory Sanderson. He does look like a surfer with that dark-blond hair, and he's pretty good at surfing and a lot of other things, now that I think about it. But his real passion is right here inside this church. He's our minister and he's good at his job. Amazing, considering he's all alone. No wife or children. Every matron in this congregation has tried to fix him up, but I think he's holding out for someone special."

Vanessa shook her head, shocked that someone so young and, well, hip, could be a preacher. "Right. Or he's so caught up in himself that he doesn't really see the audience."

"Not an audience. A congregation," Marla replied. "And you're wrong about Rory. He doesn't have an ego." She waved to a couple who sat down behind them and then pointed them out to Vanessa. "That's Alec's best friend, Blain Kent—he's also a former marine and is now a detective with the Millbrook Police—and his fiancée, Rikki Alvanetti. She's an interior designer. They're getting married in a few weeks."

Vanessa nodded and smiled at the couple. They'd make pretty babies since they both had dark hair and expressive eyes—hers almost black and his deep blue—and looked exotic and buff. And happy.

Everyone in this place seemed happy.

Chiding herself for being in such a snarky mood, she turned back to the front again. That minister seemed to be watching her. This hour couldn't get over with fast enough.

Then because she did feel guilty even thinking that, Vanessa lifted her eyes to one of the beautiful stained glass windows and asked God to give her a better perspective.

When she lowered her gaze, the cute preacher with the boyish grin and the dark-blond wind-tossed hair looked right at her and smiled. And then he did something even more daring. He came down from the front of the church and headed straight to the pew where Vanessa sat.

"Is he going to—"

"Yes, he is," Marla said with a grin. When he stopped near them, she said, "Preacher Rory, this is my friend Vanessa Donovan. She moved back to town a couple of weeks ago."

"Not moved back," Vanessa corrected. "I came back to take care of some things."

The preacher took Vanessa's hand, shaking it lightly before he stood back and smiled, his baby blue eyes centered on Vanessa as if she were the only person in this place. "It's nice to meet you, Vanessa. Welcome to Millbrook Lake Church."

"Uh…thanks," Vanessa said, a white heat of embarrassment moving up her spine. "It's nice to meet you, too."

He spoke to a few more people and then turned back to Vanessa. "Happy Easter."

She watched as he headed toward the back and greeted almost everyone else who entered the open double doors.

"He's so friendly," she whispered to Marla. "I'm not sure how to take that."

Marla glanced back and then turned to Vanessa. "You know, you need to let go of that cynical attitude. Preacher is solid. He's a good man. He was a chaplain in the army."

"What?" Vanessa looked over her shoulder. "That sunny, happy, goofy man served in the military?"

"He sure did," Marla replied. "And…he wasn't always so sunny and happy and goofy."

Faith is the substance of things hoped for…

Vanessa thought about that verse of scripture on the short ride back to Alec and Marla's house. Why did that particular verse seem to move through her like the blue waters of the big oval lake centered in the middle of town?

Maybe it wasn't the verse so much as the preacher who'd read it. Rory Sanderson didn't preach. He talked. In a quiet, friendly tone that made you think he really was talking to you and only you. Which irritated Vanessa. She didn't want to like the man, but some of what he'd said made sense.

She had listened, too. He'd pointed out how Jesus liked to hang out with the misfits and the outsiders. How a lot of those kinds of people were there during His Crucifixion.

But she had to wonder if the misfits and losers had been allowed in the church today. Everyone at the service had seemed so fresh faced and full of joy. Were they all that happy, or had they been hiding their pain behind a pretty facade?

Vanessa didn't know and it really didn't matter. She probably wouldn't go back to Millbrook Lake Church. She hadn't been to church in a long, long time. And she didn't plan on staying in Millbrook for too long either.

Clean out the house. Sell the house. Pocket the cash. Get on with her life. Whatever that life might be. Right now, she had a solid team looking out for her interests, and she had a boutique and online business waiting for her back in New Orleans. So she took a deep breath and decided she'd try to be grateful for being invited to share a nice meal with Marla's family. She could deal with other people's families, but she did not need one of her own.

Pulling her small car up to the side drive next to Caldwell House, Vanessa got out and took in the scents of jasmine and wisteria, thankful that she didn't have to spend this gorgeous day alone.

But when she looked up and saw a man strolling up the sidewalk, she silently groaned.

The preacher headed toward her. And she had the sinking feeling he would be at Sunday dinner, too.

Rory waved to the woman who emerged from the cute little blue vintage roadster. Vanessa Donovan, still wearing those shades. She'd taken them off during the service, but he had yet to see her eyes up close. He'd been too busy preaching it to a full house. Now he might be able to have some one-on-one time with the interesting woman who stood staring at him as if she wanted to get back in the car and haul herself far away from here.

"How are you?" he asked, determined to make her take off those ridiculously big shades. He was pretty sure they were missing from the 1960s, too. And maybe even the dress.

But she made all of these old-fashioned things fresh and new.

"I'm good." She held a straw purse embellished with a big white daisy that Mrs. Fitzpatrick would surely love and met him at the intricate gate to the back garden. "I...I enjoyed your sermon."

Polite but cool. "Thank you. I'm glad you made it to the service today. How do you know Marla?"

She looked relieved to move away from the topic of church. "We were friends in high school briefly and then we ran into each other in Tallahassee before I moved to New Orleans. I'm so glad she's found someone. She deserves to be happy." Then she winced. "Oh, wow. That sounded so cliché."

Rory laughed and walked with her up the steps onto the back porch. Aunt Hattie and Marla had the porch decorated with white lace tablecloths and all kinds of fresh flowers. "But it's true. Marla and Alec are meant for each other. They had their wedding reception right here in the garden, in December."

"So I heard. Sounds beautiful."

"And romantic," he said with a grin. "One of the many perks of my job. I presided over their vows. Chilly weather but warm atmosphere."

She finally took off her shades and gave him a doubting stare with big hazel eyes that went from brown to green in a beautiful flash. But before Rory could counter her skeptical expression with something positive, the back door opened and little Gabby came running out, followed by two dogs.

"Hello, Uncle Rory," Gabby said, squealing in delight as both animals ran circles around Rory and Vanessa. "Angus, stop. Roxie, quit being so silly."

Rory squatted down and smiled at Gabby, careful not to get too close. The four-year-old had the little poodle Roxie for a reason, and Roxie sometimes wore a service vest for a reason. The tiny dog was trained to keep Gabby calm whenever she felt threatened or afraid. Which happened less and less these days, thankfully. The little girl had gone through a lot of trauma after being involved in a robbery that took her daddy's life.

"Hello, Gabby," he said. "This is my new friend, Vanessa. Don't you love her pretty dress?"

Gabby grabbed Roxie and stood back to stare up at Vanessa with big brown eyes. Bobbing her head in agreement with Rory's question, she asked, "Are you eating dinner with us?"

"I am," Vanessa said, clearly uncomfortable with the whole Sunday-dinner thing. Or maybe the child made her uncomfortable. "Is that okay?"

Gabby showed a snaggletoothed grin. "Yes, ma'am. Are you hungry? We have ham and mashed potatoes and asp-per-gus. I don't like that, though."

"I don't either," Rory said, grinning. "But I love me some mashed potatoes."

"And I like ham and asparagus," Vanessa said. "I hear your mother made cupcakes and pies, too."

Gabby did a little back and forth sway, her print dress swishing. "Uh-huh. She made Easter cupcakes with bunnies and flowers and grass. I'm gonna eat two."

"And I'll eat three at least," Rory said, glad that Vanessa was warming up to the little girl. Gabby would sense it if Vanessa wasn't comfortable.

"Hello there." Aunt Hattie came strolling out, her arms wide open and her cheeky smile warm. "Welcome, welcome. I'm so glad you're both here and that you found each other out there."

"We did," Rory said, shooting Vanessa an encouraging glance. "Ran into each other by the gate."

"Did that hurt?" Gabby asked, her eyes wide again.

Aunt Hattie hooted with laughter. "Out of the mouths of babes."

"I don't know yet," Rory said, his gaze still on Vanessa. "It wasn't too painful to me. How about you, Vanessa?"

She smiled and shook her head. "We're fine, Gabby."

Then she walked with Aunt Hattie into the house, leaving Rory to wonder if *he'd* ever be fine again.

Of all the people he'd seen in church this morning, why did this woman have to be the one who'd come to dinner at the Caldwells'? And why did she have to be the one who'd left him wondering and wanting to help her when he didn't even know what she needed?

Why not?

God always put people in certain places for a reason. Vanessa was here for a reason. Rory should know better than anyone that humans didn't make their own paths.

Sometimes God put a woman in a bright yellow dress right smack-dab in the middle of the road so she could be found.

And sometimes He stopped a hopeful preacher cold in his tracks just to keep him on his toes. For a brief moment guilt gnawed at his conscience, but Rory took in the scent of flowers all around him and nodded. No matter what happened, this spring was glorious.

Chapter Two

Vanessa strolled around the big rambling backyard at Caldwell House, her mind on everything she had to get done during the next few weeks.

"Tea?"

Rory handed her a refill while they watched Gabby, with Roxie right on her heels, searching for Easter eggs in the many dish gardens and potted palms displayed all around the colorful yard.

"Thank you." Vanessa took the goblet of dark tea flavored with lemon. Not knowing what else to say, she smiled. "What a meal."

She'd enjoyed listening to the easy banter, the tiny bits of good-natured gossip and the news of the week. Millbrook Lake was growing now that the local economy had finally improved. She knew Alec had a lot to do with that since he'd returned home. She hadn't kept up much with Millbrook Lake. Mainly because she'd never planned to return here.

"I'll say." Rory rubbed his flat stomach. "I shouldn't have had pie and cupcakes, but the cooking around here is so good I always double up when I get invited for Sunday dinner."

She had to laugh. Watching him eat had been an event in itself. "Do you get invited to lunch and dinner a lot?"

"Sure. And breakfast, too. A perk of the job. People love to feed the preacher. Especially since this preacher lives alone."

She glanced over at him and saw a darkness moving through his eyes like a cloud over a clear sky. She wanted to ask him about that, but he looked straight ahead and watched Gabby with a quiet intensity that belied his cheerful nature.

"The meal was amazing," she said, suddenly unsure around him. Suddenly remembering that she had not wanted to be around him. And yet, here she stood. But she also thought about Marla's words to her earlier about him not always being so sunny, happy and goofy.

She could handle cheerful and friendly. Those were easy emotions. But imagining Rory Sanderson sad made her concerned and curious. Though wary around men of the cloth, she didn't want to think of this man as anything other than what he seemed. His carefree nature didn't appear at all threatening.

But then, she shouldn't be thinking of him anyway. He was the preacher. A man of God. Certainly not her type. Not that she was looking. She'd sworn off any long-term relationships, and she certainly wasn't ready for anything else. She thought of the tiny church up the road and willed herself to push away the memories of another church that had been located on the outskirts of town. Gone now. Torn down for new commercial real estate.

"I don't normally eat so much," she continued in the small-talk vein. "But Aunt Hattie is famous for her meals, and Marla is amazing with sugar and flour and butter."

"A dynamic duo," he said, the smile bright on his face again. "I need a long Sunday-afternoon nap."

She could picture him kicked back in a recliner, snoring softly. That did make her smile.

"I'd think you don't get to rest much," she blurted to get rid of that warm, fuzzy feeling. "I mean, being a minister."

"I get eight hours of sleep most nights, but things happen. A death, a birth, a trip to the ER, a hospital visit now and then." He gave her a quick but concise glance. "Sometimes people need to talk, even in the middle of the night."

Vanessa got that image in her head, too. Her reaching for the phone, calling him. Telling him her worst fears.

She tried again with the small talk. "And you have to be there for all of those things."

"Spoken like someone who might know."

"I don't know much," she said, her tone sharp in her own ears. She didn't like the direction this conversation seemed to be heading—toward her. "But it's obvious enough."

"I guess it is," he said, his words somber now. "My reputation precedes me."

He'd misunderstood. Most people did whenever she made disparaging remarks regarding church. But she never explained her reasons for staying away from organized religion.

She wanted to say it wasn't *his* reputation she based her assumption on, but those of other people. Only, she wasn't ready to get that personal with him. She didn't plan on being around this man after today anyway. She had plenty to keep her busy.

"You seem to be popular with your people," she said.

"*God's* people," he corrected with a smile. "I try to help them along."

They came to a big swing centered underneath an

arbor covered with jasmine. The fragrant scent of the tiny yellow-and-white flowers and the droning hum of bees made Vanessa wish for something she couldn't even define.

"Want to sit and watch the egg hunt?" he asked.

She glanced at the swing and then back at him. "I don't know. I mean, I should be going. I have a lot to do tomorrow." Needing to explain, she added, "I'm here to clean out my mother's house. She died a few weeks ago."

His expression turned compassionate. "I'm sorry. Did she live here?"

"She used to. She moved to a retirement and nursing facility in Alabama. She hadn't lived here in years."

He nodded, his expressive face couched in a calm that made him change from boyish to good-looking. "I get a day off tomorrow. If you need any help."

"I don't think so. This is one of your busy weekends. You need to rest after your big day."

"Yes. But then, I consider every Sunday a big day."

Vanessa gave him a hesitant smile. "I think I'll go and tell the others I'm leaving. It was nice to meet you—"

"Rory," he said. "Call me Rory."

She nodded and headed back to where Marla and her parents were helping Gabby find the colorful eggs. The little girl giggled and showed off her treasures while Roxie squeaked out excited barks and ran circles around the adults.

Angus watched the whole show from a warm spot on the brick terrace near the porch. The older Border collie didn't have a care in the world.

Aunt Hattie met her near the house. "We're so glad you came today, Vanessa. I hope you'll visit again."

"Thank you for inviting me," Vanessa said. "The food was so good, Aunt Hattie."

"Nothing like a home-cooked meal to nourish us, even if it does require a few extra calories."

Vanessa hadn't had many home-cooked meals growing up. "I can't argue with that." She hugged Aunt Hattie, the scent of sweet almond surrounding her. "I have to go, but I wanted to thank you again. Let me tell Marla I'm leaving."

"Oh, she wrapped you a plate," Aunt Hattie said. "I'll go fetch it."

Vanessa didn't need a plate full of leftovers, but she wouldn't be impolite by turning it down. She wasn't used to this kind of attention, and she wasn't sure how to respond. Somewhere in the back of her mind, she wished she'd had this kind of family growing up. But in that other place, the dark spot that colored her world in grays and browns, she figured she didn't deserve this kind of family.

She wished someone had trained her in proper manners or on how to actually conduct small talk. She wished she'd been happy in any of the many places her mother had dragged her. She wished she'd had nice clothes and pretty things.

And she really wished she'd had someone to truly love her.

But she couldn't change any of that now. Vanessa had learned about all of these things mostly on her own by studying people and reading books and watching television and movies. She'd learned how to dress by working in retail and devouring fashion magazines and with the help of her mother's last husband, Richard Tucker, who'd taken them on shopping trips. And she'd learned how to stay on her budget by shopping vintage and reworking second-hand clothes.

She still had to learn the truly-loving-her part. She didn't always love herself very much.

She sent Rory a brief glance and then dropped her gaze to her sandals.

"Hey, I'll come by next week and help you out with getting ready for the estate sale," Marla said as she hurried up to Vanessa. "I'll even find some able-bodied helpers to do the heavy lifting." She cast a glance toward Rory. "An estate sale is a big job."

A job Vanessa dreaded. "Yes. But…it has to be done."

"Are you gonna be okay, doing this?" Marla asked, her green eyes full of understanding and sympathy.

"I'll be fine." Vanessa glanced over to where Alec sat at a round wrought iron table with Rory. Were they actually having more cupcakes? "I have to get the house ready to sell, and I can't do that until I empty it out."

"Your mother was a pack rat from what I hear," Marla said with a smile. "I know this has been hard, Vanessa."

Vanessa nodded. "Yep. Especially since she and I never got along." She stared at the swing, where she could be sitting right now with Rory. "I guess I'll get to know her a little more now that she's dead, at least. I never could figure her out when she was alive."

"You did your best."

"I left."

It was that simple. She'd left after one divorce too many and after one particular stepfather's bad behavior. It didn't matter that her mother had tried to make amends to Vanessa after Cora had married Richard, her final husband. At least Richard had been kind to Vanessa during the short time she'd lived here with her mother and him. A good man, a very wealthy man, he'd paid off her mother's house and shown both mother and daughter a world they'd only dreamed about. He'd died five years after marrying her mother.

None of it mattered now. She couldn't live in her mother's house.

She heard the preacher's hearty laughter and stole another glance at him. "What's with him, Marla? I asked you about his story, and I'd like to know more."

Marla followed her gaze. "What makes you think he has a story?"

"We all do. You said he wasn't always this happy."

Marla shrugged. "I don't know much other than he joined the army after attending seminary, served as a chaplain and then came home to become a minister. And I don't ask beyond that. I'm not even sure Alec knows, but they have this buddy system that holds them all together and they don't press each other about what they went through while serving. I can allow that, given how I held everything inside when Alec and I started seeing each other."

"And now?"

Marla's smile was serene and sure. "And now I tell Alec everything and he shares a lot with me. We're good."

"But he doesn't talk about the preacher's past?"

"Nope. It's not his to talk about. But then, they were all over there serving our country in one capacity or another. It's a bond they share."

A bond that might not be broken, Vanessa decided. "I have to get going," she said. "I had a great time."

"I'm glad you came," Marla said. She hugged Vanessa close.

"And if you ever need to talk—"

"I'll call you," Vanessa replied. She didn't want to get emotional in front of everyone.

"Of course," Marla said. Then she inclined her chin

toward Rory. "But you should call him, too. No matter what you've been through, he's the best person to listen and help you."

"I'll keep that in mind," Vanessa replied, remembering how he'd mentioned late-night calls from his congregation members. But she said it with a smile…and a shred of hope.

A few days later, Rory worked his way around the church yard, clearing away broken limbs and picking up palm fronds. A storm had moved over the area the night before, leaving debris in its wake. He didn't mind the busywork, though. Not on a nice morning with a cool breeze pushing over the nearby waters of the lake. A few seagulls cawed at him as they came in for a low flight, probably hoping to find some morsels for breakfast.

After dropping some twigs and leaves into a nearby trash can, he stopped to look over the grounds. The little clapboard chapel had survived worse storms than this one. It was over a century old and not much bigger than a shotgun house, but the people of Millbrook Lake loved their church.

He loved it, too. Once he would have gone on by this place, but that Rory was long gone. *This* Rory loved *this* place. He stared out over the moss-draped live oaks that edged the old cemetery behind the church and prayed that he'd never have to be anywhere else.

Purple wisteria blossoms rained down each time the wind blew through the trees, their old vines wrapped like necklaces around the billowing oaks. The sound of the palms swaying in the breeze sang a comforting, serene tune. Blue jays and cardinals fussed at each other near the bird feeders one of the church members had built and hung near the pergola where people liked to hold picnics.

And the ever-present, pesky squirrels chased each other through the trees with all the precision of drag-racing champions.

What a view.

"You're not working."

He whirled to find Mrs. Fitzgerald standing with her flower-encased walker near the sidewalk, her hat today black straw with red cherries around the rim.

"I'm taking a thankful break," he explained with a grin.

"Can I come and take it with you?" she asked. "I'm thankful and I have corn fritters."

Rory brushed his hands against his old jeans. "Bring yourself on over to this picnic table," he said. "How did you know I had a hankering for corn fritters this morning?"

She gave him a mock scowl, her wrinkles folding against each other, her gray hair as straw-like as her hat. "Since when have you *not* been hankering for something to eat? I declare, I don't know how you stay so fit."

"I pick up limbs and trash all the time," he said with a deadpan expression.

"Yes, you do. And you ride that bicycle and carry that board thing out to the water." She moseyed over to the table and fluffed her yellow muumuu. "You swim and fish and surf and jog all over the place. When do you rest, Preacher?"

"I'll rest when I die."

She shook her head. "Oh, I doubt that. The Lord will put you straight to work when you reach the Pearly Gates."

They both laughed at that notion. Then she pulled out the still-warm corn fritters that were her specialty. Part hush puppy and part corn bread, the fat mushy balls were filled with real corn nuggets and tasted like nectar to Rory.

"So good," he said. "I think I'll be able to finish this mess before lunch, thanks to you."

Mrs. Fitzgerald chewed on her food and studied the water. "Nice sermon yesterday. I think you impressed that newcomer."

Miss Fanny, as she liked to be called, took impish pleasure in stirring the pot.

Rory played coy. "We had a newcomer?"

The older woman playfully slapped his arm. "I saw you looking at her. And I'm pretty sure she was looking back."

"Don't you have cataracts?"

"Not since that fancy eye doctor up on 98 did some sort of surgery on me. I can see a feather caught in a limb up in that tree yonder."

He glanced at the tree and squinted. "Feathers are a bit different from watching me and making assumptions."

"I know what I see," she replied on a prim note. "It's springtime. Love is in the air."

"Well, aren't you the poet."

"I used to be, you know."

"You? A poet?" Miss Fanny was full of surprises.

"Me." She pointed to the houses lining the lake. "See that Craftsman cottage with the blue shutters?"

He nodded and grabbed another fritter. "The one near your house that's in need of serious repair?"

She lived in a small Cape Cod style two-storied house across from the church.

"That's the one. I used to run around with the woman who lived there. We were artists. She dabbled in mixed media and men. I dabbled in poetry and one long and loving marriage."

"You don't say?" He'd heard about how much Miss Fanny loved her husband, but she was already a widow when he met her. "So what happened to your friend? That house has been vacant since I've been here."

"That was her home at one time, but after she remarried, it became a vacation home. The last man she married also had a home in Birmingham, Alabama, and they used to travel back and forth. But…she died recently." Fanny took off her hat and gave him a direct stare. "That woman you're pretending you didn't notice in church yesterday, that's her daughter. She's come back here to fix up and sell the house." Putting her hat back on, she added, "Vanessa hated her mother. And I might as well tell you she's not too fond of preachers either."

Chapter Three

Rory stood up to stare over at the rambling one-story house with the blue shutters. Well, the shutters used to be blue. Now they were a peeling, weathered blue-gray mess. The whole place wore a facade of neglect even though the neighbors kept the yard mowed and the flower beds pruned and trimmed, as a courtesy and in keeping with the pretty factor that Millbrook Lake prided itself on.

So that was the house Vanessa had mentioned the other day. And Miss Fanny had been a friend to her deceased mother.

"I've often thought someone needed to buy that place and fix it up," he said. "So that's where Vanessa Donovan used to live?"

And now she was back.

"Her mother lived there for years, but Vanessa only lived there for a couple of years after Cora and Richard got married and moved here. She finished high school and then she left. To my knowledge, this is the first time she's been back."

Rory thought about how long the house had sat vacant. "But somebody kept up with the place. I mean, it's still full of furniture and belongings."

Miss Fanny sat staring across at the house. "Cora, Vanessa's mother, went to a nursing home in Alabama near where her last husband had property, right before you came to town. After Vanessa graduated high school, Richard and Cora split their time between Birmingham and here. Then after he died, Cora came back here. But she got sick and that ended, so she moved to a retirement home that had around-the-clock nursing. We all tried to keep the house ready for her to come back, but she never recovered from her first stroke. She had another massive one about a month ago and died. Buried in Alabama beside the one man she truly loved." Miss Fanny's shrug was eloquent. "Maybe because he left her a ton of money. She never talked much about the men in her life, but Richard was very special to her."

Suddenly, Rory understood a lot of things. "So Vanessa came back to…settle things?"

"That's an understatement," Miss Fanny replied. "The girl inherited the house and probably some money and other property, too. But I'm thinking she won't want to live here. She'll probably sell out and leave again." Miss Fanny leaned close. "Vanessa loved her mother's last husband, Richard Tucker. He was like a true father to her after so many other men, but Vanessa and Cora did not see eye-to-eye about anything. Too many bad memories."

Rory thought about the woman he'd first noticed in church last Sunday. Afraid and unsure and wound as tight as fishing line on a reel. Yeah, he could see a lot of *settling things* needed to occur.

And he had to ask. "Why does Vanessa dislike preachers, Miss Fanny?"

Miss Fanny got up and adjusted her hat. "I'll give you one guess."

Rory closed his eyes and lowered his head. "Which husband was it?"

"Number three," Miss Fanny said without missing a beat. "Vanessa was around thirteen or fourteen, I think, when her mother married a minister from Atlanta. They moved here since she already had this house. He served a church out on the highway for a couple of years. Neither his assignment nor the marriage lasted. But while he was here, he tried to *reform* Vanessa but in the worst sort of way."

Giving Rory a pointed glance, she started pushing her walker toward the street, Rory following while he kept his gaze on the house. "Her mother sided with the preacher, of course."

The rich fritters Rory had woofed down now felt like lead inside his stomach. He had to wonder what Vanessa had been through, how much she'd suffered. He didn't ask. Miss Fanny probably knew, but he wouldn't ask her to tell him.

Vanessa would have to be the one to do that.

If she ever trusted him enough to tell him anything.

"Let me walk you to your door," he told Miss Fanny. He needed to think this through. He checked the driveway next door to see if Vanessa's little blue car was parked there.

"She's not there," Miss Fanny said, already reading his mind. "I think she went to the lawyer's office to take care of some business. Probably the reading of the will." The older woman turned when they reached her front porch steps. "But she's planning a big estate sale sometime soon. She'll need help...sorting through all that clutter."

She shrugged. "And since you're also planning a rummage sale at the church…"

Rory nodded. "I'll be glad to help."

Miss Fanny nodded, her work here done.

"Thank you for the corn fritters," Rory said after he'd made sure she was safe back inside her house. "Go take your afternoon nap."

Miss Fanny waved him away and shut the door.

Rory hurried back down the steps, but he stopped on the sidewalk and glanced over at the long, sprawling house to the left of Miss Fanny's place.

He hadn't said this to Miss Fanny, but Rory had often thought he'd like to buy the old Craftsman cottage and fix it up.

But now, he also had the added challenge of trying to help repair the woman who'd come to town to sell this house. He'd have to pray hard on how to manage that without scaring Vanessa away for good. And he'd have to pray hard for her to forgive the minister who'd obviously damaged her for life.

"What did you say?"

Vanessa stared at the studious gray-haired lawyer sitting across from her in the elegant conference room situated in an old Georgian-style building across town.

Charles Barton leaned up and studied Vanessa's face, his bifocal glasses low on his hawk-like nose. "I said you have inherited the bulk of Richard Tucker's estate. Mind you, after your mother's care and expenses over the last few years, a fourth of it is gone. But you have the Millbrook Lake cottage and you have the holdings in Alabama, namely a house in Birmingham and several commercial rental properties in that area."

Vanessa sat staring at the man across from her, unable to comprehend what he was telling her. Finally, she swallowed and spoke. "I knew Richard left my mother comfortable, and I was grateful that she had constant, around-the-clock care at the nursing facility, but I had no idea about something such as this happening."

When Mr. Barton had stated the exact amount of the inheritance, Vanessa had almost fallen out of her chair. Growing up, she'd often dreamed of that kind of money. Now, she was content with her shop in New Orleans and the online boutique full of eclectic clothes and artisan wares from hundreds of vendors. She wasn't rich by any means, but she made a good living, selling quirky items to quirky people. Vanessa's Vintage had taken off in the last year or so. The boutique in New Orleans had become popular with both locals and tourists, and the online store kept up a steady business.

"You are now a wealthy young woman," the lawyer stated. "Of course, we'll deal with probate and a few other minor details, but all in all, since Richard had no other close relatives, this should be an easy transition."

"I'd planned to clean up the cottage and sell it," Vanessa admitted, still numb. "I thought that was the only thing I needed to worry about."

"You can decide what to sell off and what to keep once this sets in," Mr. Barton said. "After a death, I always tell my clients who are left to take over estates not to make any rash decisions. Give it some time. You're still working through a lot of emotions."

The older man's soft-spoken advice calmed Vanessa. "You're right. I have a lot to do back at the cottage. Getting the place cleaned up and renovated to sell will give me time to decide where I go from here."

"Do you think you'll want to keep the mansion in Birmingham?" he asked.

Vanessa thought about the stately Tudor-style house sitting up on a remote bluff. "It's a beautiful house, but I never actually lived there. I visited a few times, but I can't see me living in that big, old house."

Mr. Barton's assistant began gathering files and folders. He stood, too, and waited for Vanessa to do the same. "Take your time. The money and holdings won't be going anywhere and there are trustworthy people in place to take care of things."

Vanessa thanked the lawyer and left, thinking she wouldn't be going anywhere for a while either. She now had a lot more to take care of than she'd ever imagined.

But for now, she'd focus on the cottage.

She drove around the lake and circled back toward Lake Street, where all the quaint Victorian houses sat next to the few Cape Cod homes and the other one-story Craftsman cottages that were scattered throughout. The view across the water was breathtaking and beautiful.

Until she spotted her house.

The cottage looked sad and lonely, neglected.

That mirrored how she'd felt most of her life. This house held a strong pull over her, one that she needed to resist and one she'd managed to avoid up until now.

Ironic that now she had the security and wealth she'd always craved but she didn't have anyone to share it with.

Her mother had finally found her fairy tale with Richard Tucker, but it hadn't lasted. He'd died a year after Vanessa left to go to college.

Vanessa had never wanted a fairy tale. She'd only wanted a family. They'd had that with Richard. He'd been kind and gracious and so patient with her mother's temperamental mood swings and crazy impulsive nature. He'd also taken time with Vanessa, showing her proper decorum and giving her instructions on manners and how to win over even her worst critics. But he'd done it all in a caring, loving way that made Vanessa feel treasured and special.

Not ashamed and embarrassed.

Still in shock from the lawyer's news, she drove on around the lake and pulled up into the driveway of her house. When she got out of the car, she glanced toward the church and wondered what Rory was doing. Marla had told Vanessa that he lived in a small garage apartment behind the church. Maybe he *would* be a good person to talk to in confidence about her situation.

But then again, maybe not. She was leery of showing him any signs of weakness even if he didn't seem the type to take advantage of her.

She wouldn't be pulled into something she'd regret. She couldn't be fooled into getting too close to organized religion again. She believed in God, but she was afraid of putting too much trust in people. The pain of her last encounter with a man of God still gave her nightmares.

She couldn't go through that again.

No matter how much she needed a friend.

Rory went on with his day. It was nearly sundown now, so he finished up the yard work behind the church, careful to stay out of sight of the house across the street. But it hadn't been easy to stay away after the heavy hints Miss Fanny had dropped regarding Vanessa's past.

Usually when a visitor came to church, some of the welcome committee members would take over a basket full of books, cookies, gift certificates to local establishments and ground coffee from Marla's place with a cute Millbrook Lake Church mug sporting a pelican sitting on a pew with the caption *Don't fly by. Come on in.*

Sometimes, he'd tag along on these welcome visits.

Not this time.

It wasn't that he didn't want to reach out to Vanessa. But he'd counseled enough members of the military to know that when someone didn't want to listen, it was hard to talk to them. Rory had his ways of helping people to find their faith, and those ways didn't involve being pushy and too in-your-face. He'd have to bide his time with Vanessa Donovan. He'd seen people hurt by those who used their own agenda in the name of the Lord.

It was never pretty.

So now, he raked and prayed and raked some more and tried to think about what he could have for dinner. Maybe he'd go to the Back Bay Pizza House and order a takeout meatball sub. Or maybe he'd swing by the Courthouse Café and get a big hamburger and fries before they shut down for the day. Or he could pull out his bike and ride around the lake and stop at the Fish Barrel, the new alfresco dining truck that offered up some really good grouper sandwiches, shrimp baskets and other local fare.

He was leaning toward the bike ride and the grouper sandwich when he heard a low, feminine groan echoing out over the street. Then he heard a thump and a crash, followed by another groan and the word "Ouch."

Dropping his rake, Rory peeped around the corner of the storage shed behind the church and saw Vanessa standing in the front yard by an old wheelbarrow full of trash. He watched as she tried to move the wheelbarrow, but one of the wheels had obviously gone flat. The weight of the trash wasn't helping matters.

That old thing wasn't going to go anywhere except—

Onto its side.

It toppled over with a shudder of regret, causing another loud crash to reverberate up and down the street. Old glassware, plates, cups and other knickknacks spilled all over the driveway and sidewalk. And another groan of frustration followed.

Okay, now he had to walk over there because he had to be gallant and helpful, didn't he?

"Need some help?" he called, to show he was only trying to be a gentleman.

She glanced around, surprise brightening her shimmering eyes. Surprise, followed by what might be dread. "I'm beyond help."

"I wouldn't say that," he told her, his hands on his hips. "But…this wheelbarrow is beyond anything. I hope these dishes weren't important."

She stared at the shattered mess lying at her feet. "No, not really." But she picked up what looked like a children's cup that had colorful princess characters on it. "Just stuff my mom had shoved into the garage out back. She was a bit of a hoarder."

Rory heard the pain behind that comment. And saw that pain reflected in Vanessa's eyes while she moved her fingers over the faded little plastic cup. "Was that yours?" he asked as an opening.

She nodded. "Once, long ago."

"Where were you taking these things?"

"Out to the curb." She tossed the cup back onto the pile. "I thought someone might come by and take them."

He gave her time to get past what she had to be thinking. It must be hard to let go of so many memories. "Let me help you get this cleaned up."

She waved him away. "You don't have to do that."

"I have nothing else to do," he said. "I've been doing yard work, and I was about to quit for the day."

She glanced at the church and then back at him, the struggle in her mind evident in her brooding expression.

"I guess I could use some help," she said. "I have to

clean this place up, and that shed is just the beginning. I want to put a lot of the items from the estate sale out there, on display."

"Are you hiring an estate-sale manager?"

Her dark eyebrows shot up. "I hadn't planned on that since this is what I do for a living." She stopped and stared at the little cup.

"You work as an estate-sale manager?"

"No, but I run a vintage shop in New Orleans and an online shopping site. Vanessa's Vintage."

"Then you do know what you're doing. We're planning a rummage sale at the church in a few weeks, and one of our members used to be an estate-sale manager. She offered her services free to us. But we could coordinate things with your sale. Maybe hold them on the same day since we're neighbors." He stopped, waited a couple of beats. When she didn't scowl at him, he added, "That is, if you're okay with that idea."

She glanced at the church, and then she looked down at the old wheelbarrow. "I don't know. I hope I'll be gone in a few weeks."

"Forget I suggested it," Rory said. "You have too much on your mind to add a church rummage sale to the mix."

"It's okay," she replied, pushing at her shoulder-length wavy bob. "I don't know what I'm doing, really. I mean, I know vintage and collectibles, but I've never done this before. But I always managed to figure things out on my own."

He picked up the princess cup. "Well, now you're not on your own. You have help. Starting with me."

She stared over at him, her gaze moving from his face to the pile of broken dishes. "And what's in it for you, Preacher?"

Chapter Four

"**W**hat do you mean?"

Rory tried the tactic he used whenever someone asked him a disconcerting question. And prayed it would work on Vanessa.

She gave him a surprised glance, her brow furrowing. "It's a simple question. You're offering to help me. You must have a reason."

"Wow. Does there have to be a reason?" Not sure how to handle this kind of skepticism, he leaned his head down and gave her a smile. "Part of my job is to help others. Part of my nature is to be sincere about it."

She actually blushed. "I'm sorry. I shouldn't have said that. I've had a trying day and I have trust issues."

He widened the smile. "You think?"

She shook her head and shot him a wry grin. "I guess I should loosen up, right?"

"No. Don't do anything on my account. This ain't my first rodeo."

She laughed at that. "You look too young and carefree to be a preacher."

He thought of the man who'd obviously hurt her. "Ministers come in all shapes and sizes. And personalities."

"Yeah, you can say that again."

He stuffed the cup inside one of the deep pockets of his baggy work shorts and started picking up the broken dishes in an effort to distract her. "Hey, if you find me a broom and a dustpan, I can get this done a lot quicker. And then I'll be happy to buy you a cup of coffee or a cold drink."

"So you can work me over?"

That skeptical imp again, hiding serious pain. "Work you over?"

She started walking backward toward the big shed beyond the open gate to the backyard. "You know, telling me that God loves me and that He can make things better for me?"

"Of course," Rory said, stooping to pick up the bigger pieces of shattered porcelain. "That's part of my job, too."

She turned and hurried. "At least you're not trying to slip it under the radar."

"Nope. I'm not that kind of guy," he called after her. When she kept walking, he called louder. "What you see is what you get with me. It's pretty much the same with God, too."

He glanced up to find an older couple across the street with their dog watching him with a curious regard.

"Oh, hi," Rory called. "Nice day, don't you think?"

They nodded, waved and hurried away. The little dog, however, woofed a quick reply.

No wonder they'd moved on. He seemed to be talking to himself.

Worried that Vanessa had run off in the other direction, he stood and checked the open gate. Maybe she'd gone inside the house to find the broom and dustpan.

Rory cleaned up a bit more and then decided to check on Vanessa. He strolled through the open wrought iron gate and searched the big backyard. Lots of vintage patio furniture and nice palm trees and old oaks, but no Vanessa.

Turning toward the big shed she'd talked about, Rory went to the open French doors. "Hey, Vanessa, you in here?"

He found her standing at a table, her hand on an open book. A photo album from what he could tell.

When he moved toward her, she whirled, her gaze locking with his. "I'm sorry. I…I can't find the dustpan."

Rory walked over to where she stood. "Do you want me to leave?"

She nodded and then she shook her head no. "I…I don't want you to leave but…I can't… I'm not ready for this."

"Not ready for me and my poor attempts to comfort you? Or not ready to clean out this house?"

"Not ready for…accepting that my mother is gone," she said. Then she sniffed and wiped at her eyes. "I'll clean up the mess out front later. You…you don't have to hang around."

Rory wasn't going to leave her like this. "Nonsense. You go in the house and have a good cry or make yourself a cup of tea or eat ice cream. I see the broom over there, and I can use the lid off this old box as a dustpan. I'll clean up the broken things out front."

She gave him a confused stare, her eyes misty with a raw-edged pain. "You don't have to clean up my mess."

Rory wondered how many times she'd said that to other people. "I don't mind."

She nodded, grabbed the photo album and pushed past him for the door. But she turned once she was outside. "Thank you, Rory."

He nodded and smiled at her. "Hey, listen. Grief is

a sneaky thing. One minute you're doing fine and the next, you want to punch something. Or…break dishes."

She smiled through her tears. "I guess I've done that already today."

She turned and ran toward the house, her flip-flops hitting against the steps up to the back porch. He watched her until he heard the door slam.

Rory tore off the box top and took it and the broom back up to the sidewalk and began to clear away the debris. But in his heart, he wanted to go inside that house and help clear up the debris of Vanessa's broken heart. Because he didn't have enough prayers to give her the kind of comfort she craved and needed.

And yet, he knew the comfort of God's love.

So he prayed anyway, until he had the yard clean again.

He'd have to keep working on the woman sitting inside, crying over an old photo album. And he'd have to do it in a gentle way that would help her to heal.

Vanessa wished she hadn't fallen apart in front of the preacher. Now he'd really want to talk to her. She only wanted to sit here and stare into space. But she had so much to take care of before she could go back to New Orleans.

Her fingers touched on an old photograph of her mother with Vanessa on a beach blanket, forcing her to remember the good times. They'd been few and far between, but she had brief flashes of laughter and sunshine and a warm feeling.

A feeling of being loved. Had she forgotten the good and focused too much on the bad? The pictures in this album only showed smiling faces and what looked like good times.

Why were there never any pictures of the bad times? Never any proof of how she remembered things? No, those things had been hidden away, swept underneath the heavy carpet in a facade that was hard to pull away.

A soft knock at the back door brought her head up. Vanessa wiped at her eyes and shut the old photo album. Then she rushed to the door and opened it to find Rory standing there with two ice cream cones.

"The truck came by," he said, smiling. "I like chocolate and I got you caramel-vanilla. But if you don't want it—"

She grabbed the waffle cone and took a small nip. "Oh."

"I take that as a yes." He ate some of his and glanced around. "Nice house."

"Come in," she said, her mind still on the caramel-vanilla.

He stepped inside, and Vanessa realized no one had been invited inside this house in a long time. Shame and embarrassment hit at her with the same freezing intensity as the ice cream sliding down her throat. The built-in cabinets on each side of the enormous fireplace were true to the Craftsman style of the house. But the shelves were practically groaning with old books and side-by-side knick-knacks. Not to mention stacks of newspapers and scraps of all kinds of fabric remnants lying here and there in front of the shelves.

"It's a mess," she said, lifting her free hand in the air. "One room at a time. I keep telling myself that's how I'll get it done."

Rory glanced around, his gaze settling on the folded blanket and bed pillow she'd left on the couch. She didn't want to explain that she'd slept in here last night.

But Rory didn't mention what had to be obvious. Instead, he said, "So…are you going to sell off everything in here?"

"Not everything all at once," she said. "I have my on-line vintage store, so I'll place some of the items there." She ate more ice cream, the cold sweetness making her feel better. "And if you're serious about me having the estate sale when you have the church rummage sale, then I'll probably get rid of a lot of the bigger pieces there, since shipping them is kind of costly."

"Of course I'm serious. If you don't mind staying a week or so longer than you planned. We hope to hold it sometime in May, but I'll pin the committee people down on an exact date."

"That would help," she replied. "A deadline will force me to stop procrastinating and get this over with."

And what could a few more weeks hurt? She could handle this. She had to get this house on the market, and she couldn't do that until she had it cleaned up and spruced up.

"Then it's settled. We can go over the details in the next week or so," he said. "The church members will appreciate having the draw of an estate sale next door." He walked around, studying the house. "This place has good bones, you know."

And a few good memories. She needed to focus on those, instead of the bad ones she'd experienced here as a teenager.

"It is a classic house," she admitted. "It needs someone to love it enough to save it."

"I think you're right," Rory said, his warm, sunny gaze moving over her face.

Vanessa tried to ignore how his nearness made her feel kind of gooey inside, so she forced herself to see it from someone else's perspective. Her mother had been an artist, dabbling in collages and mixed media. Cora Donovan Tucker never threw anything away. So every nook and cranny, every shelf and table, held what her mother had considered treasures. A feather here, an old button there. Tarnished jewelry with missing rhinestones, old purses with worn handles, books of every shape and size, yellowed with age. Clothes, dishes, trinkets. Cora had collected husbands in much the same way. Tarnished, washed up, broken people. Losers, except for Richard. He'd been a true Godsend.

Her mother had always been a work in progress. But even ravished by two strokes and unable to speak, Cora had died with a peaceful look on her face. Thankful that she'd made it to the nursing home in time to be with her mother at the end, Vanessa wondered what she'd left unsaid.

Rory picked up an object here and studied a piece of art there. "Interesting collection."

"A lot of stuff, huh?" she said, wondering what Rory really thought. Wondering why she'd let him in. *Really* let him in.

"Yes." He munched on his waffle cone. "But that's not your fault. And you don't have to go through it alone."

"Do you mean clearing away this clutter or grieving?"

He gave her that blue-eyed stare that left her feeling light and heavy at the same time. "Yes."

"I don't need a lot of help," she replied, panicking. The cold ice cream burned at her stomach. She imagined him being here every day, watching her, checking on her, asking her pointed, preacher-type questions. "I can handle this, Preacher."

He didn't speak. He kept munching on his cone. Finally, he finished chewing and nodded. "I don't doubt that, but why should you have to do this alone?"

"Why are you so determined to make sure I get help?"

He seemed to accept that she was turning ugly again, and Vanessa felt ashamed at herself. "I'm sorry. I guess I need some more time to process this."

"Okay." He finished his ice cream and went to the kitchen sink to wash his hands. "And I should leave you alone to do this in your own way."

If he noticed the dishes everywhere or the half-eaten sandwich she'd left on the counter, he didn't blink. Instead, he dried his hands on a butterfly-embossed dish towel and walked over to where she stood holding a melting ice cream cone.

"Appetite gone?" he asked, taking the cone from her.

"Yes."

He took her ice cream and went back to the sink and dropped the dripping cone inside and washed his hands again. Then he came back to stand near her. "You do what you need to do. We're all here, though. Remember that. Miss Fanny next door—she knew your mom. She's willing to help, and she's willing to listen."

"I don't need anyone to listen to me," Vanessa retorted, needing him to leave. Needing to be away from his soft, sweet gaze. "I... I'll figure this out."

"I believe you will."

"But you'd like it better if I opened up and told you all my troubles and my fears?"

He started backing toward the door. "No, I wouldn't like that better. I wouldn't like that at all. But what I would like is for you to stop seeing me as the enemy and let me be your friend."

"I can't do that," she said, tears burning at her eyes. "I don't think you're the enemy, but I can't be your friend, Rory."

He held a hand on the doorknob. "Or you can't let *me*

be your friend? Because I'm what you consider a pushy minister?"

"That's part of it. That especially, and you being so nice and *not* being a pushy minister in the way that I know, is really messing with my head."

"I wish you'd reconsider things," he said, "but I understand. I'll see you soon, I guess. You know where to find me if you need me." He opened the door, but turned back. "But *you* need to understand, I didn't come over here today to badger you. I came because I saw someone in need. That's my nature as a human being, not only as a minister. Sometimes, people tend to overlook that I'm as human as they are."

And then he was gone, just like that.

For a split second, Vanessa wanted to run after him and tell him all of her troubles. But she had to be strong. She had to fight that notion with all her being. She'd told a minister her innermost secrets before, and that man had used her fears and her insecurities against her. Never again.

She'd been taking care of herself for a long time now. Why should that change? Why should she believe a sweet-talking preacher who brought her ice cream and made her feel safe?

She rushed to the sink and turned on the hot water and watched as the caramel-vanilla ice cream melted into nothing. Her confusing thoughts about Rory had to melt into nothing, too. Because growing close to him would be a bad idea all the way around.

Why should she believe him? Why did she *want* to believe him?

Because Rory was different. She could tell that. He'd never been through the type of horrible, mortifying things she'd endured. He was happy and settled and well-rounded and content.

He didn't know the kind of pain she knew.

Did he?

Chapter Five

Rory sat behind his desk, a spot he tried not to occupy very often. He much preferred being up and about, talking to people one-on-one. Paperwork always made him antsy and tired, but today was Monday.

Paperwork day.

He signed a few more checks and went over some notes for the committee meeting he had to attend later in the week. Then he checked his watch. Blain and Rikki were coming in today to go over the last-minute details of their upcoming wedding.

Thankful that they'd managed to get past her family's alleged criminal activities and that Blain had saved her from some nasty people, Rory was glad that Blain, a detective, had fallen for Rikki, the daughter of a reputed Mafia boss. Rikki had made peace with her family since she'd found out her powerful father had truly mended his ways long ago, and Blain had made peace with his father, a retired sheriff who'd helped him crack the case.

Rory's heart warmed at the harmony all around him. Another win for the good guys.

Now he was in charge of yet another wedding. He'd

married off Alec Caldwell and Marla Hamilton right before Christmas of last year. They were thriving.

He wanted that for Blain and Rikki, too.

He might even want that again for himself one day. But he tried not to think about the past or his own heartache too much. Rory didn't talk about that time in his life. He'd been so happy, so ready to start his career as a minister. But then, his life had changed in one quick heartbeat.

People would be surprised to know he'd had to crawl out of his own dark place.

He stopped reading over the budget report and glanced out the office window, across the street to the Craftsman cottage. And wondered for the hundredth time how Vanessa was doing. She hadn't come back to church yet. But it had been only a week. He'd hoped she'd come yesterday, but he hadn't seen her in the congregation. He hadn't talked to her since the day he'd helped her with the pile of broken dishes. But he kept that little kiddie cup she'd almost tossed right here in his desk drawer so he could return it to her one day.

When she was ready.

He had a good vantage point to keep an eye on her. He'd seen her coming and going, taking boxes to the trash, loading her tiny car with bags of stuff. She was busy. She was avoiding him. Maybe she was avoiding the whole world.

He'd also seen her staring off into space, sometimes up at the house, sometimes out toward the lake. And a couple of times, over toward the church.

He prayed she'd walk over and see him one day soon. *In God's own time.*

Some people believed you had to rush right in and grab people by the lapels to convince them that God loved them. Rory preferred to let people come to that notion on their own.

So he prayed them into taking the next step. And he'd been doing a lot of praying for Vanessa lately. She was going through a deep pain, no doubt. No one here really knew he'd been through that kind of pain. Not even his best friends.

Rory wanted to keep it that way. He couldn't let people see beyond his good-natured, friendly attitude. He'd hidden that side of himself away for so long, it didn't match anymore.

He'd scare people and confuse them if he told them about the man he used to be. Not that he'd ever been scary. But he didn't want to go back to that dark spot in his soul. Ever. He'd come a long way to get to this place, and he liked his work and his life. No way did he want to go back.

And yet, when he saw his friends finding true love, he wanted to go back. He wanted to fall in love again. But at times, the bitterness reared its ugly head, and he felt envy and anger pushing at his hard-fought-for peace.

So he understood what Vanessa was fighting.

A knock at his partially open office door brought Rory out of his musings. His secretary, Barbara Rowan, peeped inside. "Hey, you awake in here?"

Rory grinned. "Barely. It's too pretty outside to be in here pushing a pencil."

Barbara, petite, with a brown bob and a blunt attitude, put her hands on her hips and gave him a mock stare, her flamingo lapel pin blinking at him in shades of pink bling. "Well, I feel so bad for you, stuck in this stuffy old office. But you have company. Blain and Rikki are here."

"Oh, right." Rory glanced at the clock again. "Send them in. This will make my day better."

Barbara nodded and opened the door wide. "Here they are."

Rory grinned at seeing Blain and Rikki holding hands, smiles on their faces. "Hello, you two."

Blain shook his hand and Rikki hugged him. "We're here for the premarital counseling you suggested," Rikki said.

"Did I suggest that?" He chuckled and motioned to the floral chairs across from his desk. "So a few more weeks, huh?"

Blain nodded, his dark blue eyes moving over his bride. "Yes. Wedding here in the church and reception out at the Alvanetti estate."

"Got it marked in red," Rory said. "Any questions?"

Rikki gave Blain a sweet smile. "How do we get past everything we went through? I mean, I've forgiven my family but…how do Blain and I keep my family issues out of our marriage?"

Blain squeezed her hand and glanced at Rory. "We want to make this work. We love each other but sometimes the world can get in the way."

Rory loved his friend Blain and he liked Rikki, too. So he leveled with them. "It's not easy. But loving each other is the first line of defense. Loving the Lord helps. Your faith is important, and that shows with you two. Be open and honest with each other, of course. Seek help when you need to. I'm always here for either of you, and I won't repeat anything said in this room. But you need to talk to your families, too. And other friends you can trust."

He glanced out the window and saw Vanessa getting into her car. She was wearing a colorful patterned sundress and tall, strappy sandals. When he glanced back at Blain and Rikki, Blain was giving him a one-eyebrow-lifted knowing stare.

Rory tried to cover. "And...uh...you should be honest with your families, too. Don't hold grudges. Talk things out. Remember the good times and try to get past the bad."

He groaned inwardly. He was talking in clichés today.

After a few more questions, he went over the wedding arrangements with them and gave them some pamphlets and books to read. They both asked more questions, and Rory said a prayer with them. "I think you two will be fine."

Blain glanced at Rikki. "Can you visit with Barbara for a minute? I need to ask Rory something."

"Sure." She gave him a brown-eyed smile, her long dark hair flowing around her shoulders. "Already keeping secrets."

"It's more guy stuff," Blain said. "Regarding my bachelor party."

"Oh, right." She grinned at Rory and went into the reception area.

"What's up?" Rory asked, his mind still on Vanessa. "You know we're having a low-key party out at the camp house, right?"

Blain laughed. "Yes, I know all about that, surprises not withstanding."

"Okay, did you need something else?"

"Are you scouting the house across the street for a reason?"

Blain was on to him. "I might be since it's going up for sale soon. I've always liked that house, and it's near the church." He shrugged. "I'm outgrowing my tiny one-bedroom apartment."

"Right." Blain rolled his eyes. "I was referring to the woman living there, not the house. Preacher, do you have your eye on Vanessa Donovan?"

Rory didn't want to squirm underneath the scrutiny of Blain's eagle-eyed gaze. "She's in a bad way, so I've tried to befriend her. Offer her my help and advice."

Blain nodded. "It's amazing. All these years, I've never seen you go beyond being friends with a woman. You don't even date. But since Vanessa rolled into town, you've seemed distracted."

"How do you know that?" Rory asked, affronted. "You haven't been around me that much when women are nearby."

"Relax," Blain said. "I saw you on Easter Sunday, and Alec told me you and Vanessa seemed chummy at Easter dinner at his house."

Rory laughed. "What you and Alec call chummy, I call being friendly."

"Oh, okay. We'll go with that then," Blain said. "It's nice to know you're human after all. You could do worse. She's cute, and Rikki says she's nice, too."

Rory rubbed a hand over his choppy hair. "Really? I hadn't noticed."

Blain shook his head. "Right. I'll shut up now. Are we still on for pizza Thursday night?"

"As always."

"And we are gathering at the camp house for my bachelor party in two weeks?"

"You better believe it. And I *do* have surprises lined up for you."

"What? Choir rehearsal and memorizing Bible verses?"

"After we play a serious game of tic-tac-toe, yes."

"Wild night. Love it." Blain shook Rory's hand and headed to the door. "Hey, Alec and I, we've been there. We should be the ones giving *you* advice these days."

Rory finally caved. "I might take you up on that offer. I like her. A lot. But…she's not returning that feeling."

"Give her some time," Blain suggested. "Like you said, she's been through a lot. One thing I've learned, dealing with Rikki and her family, strong women don't like to be messed with until they're ready to be messed with."

"Got it," Rory said, grinning at Blain's down-to-earth assessment. "I'm learning that, my friend."

After Blain and Rikki left, he turned to Barbara. "Please tell me it's quitting time."

"It's quitting time," she said. "You know you officially have Mondays off, so why are you still here?"

He shrugged. "Habit." Then he went back in his office and tidied up. "I think I've signed all the proper checks and documents so yes, I'm taking off early. I might take a run around the lake or maybe go kayaking."

"Great idea," his secretary called back. "Me, I'm going to go home and piddle in my garden."

"Okay. See you tomorrow."

Barbara left by the side door.

Rory locked up and was about to head to the garage underneath his apartment to get his kayak out when he saw Vanessa's car moving up Lake Drive.

She was home.

He was standing by his garage apartment.

Glad she was wearing her shades, Vanessa noticed Rory out of the corner of her eye. She'd tried not to think about him, but he seemed to be front and center in her mind. Reminding herself that he did live and work right across the street, she chalked up this preoccupation with the cute preacher to being in such close proximity to him. Hard not to think about him when the pretty white church stood as a reminder every time she looked out the window.

So she pulled her car into the drive and geared up for a warm, soothing bath and a bowl of ice cream. Yes, she'd been craving ice cream all week. His fault, too. But she'd had a long day of talking to lawyers and discussing things on the phone with Realtors both here in Millbrook and at the various properties she now owned in Alabama.

Overwhelmed, she glanced back toward the church.

And saw Rory heading straight for her.

She almost ran into the house, but her heart stopped her. She couldn't be rude to the man. He'd been nothing but kind to her. The least she could do was say hello to him.

Hello. And then on to ice cream.

"Hi," he called when she turned and waved. Then he walked over. Did he seem relieved?

"Hello," she replied, smiling. "How are you?"

"Good. I'm calling it a day," he said. His dark blond hair was in a perpetual state of shagginess, but it suited him. "I'm going kayaking. Wanna come?"

Kayaking? The thought of putting on shorts and a sleeveless top made her cringe. The sun had not touched her legs all winter. Did she have the nerve to actually relax and go for a ride on the lake? With him?

He must have sensed her hesitation. "I'm sorry. You're probably really busy."

She glanced at the glistening water and then gazed at him. "I've been going nonstop all day dealing with my inheritance, but that water looks so tempting."

And so did he. Not what you'd expect. Better than ice cream even.

"I have an extra kayak. It's actually Alec's, but he

won't mind if you want to use it. He stores it over here so some of the kids I mentor can borrow it."

"You mentor kids?"

He nodded and looked sheepish. "Yes. Mostly teens. We have a get-together here at the church once a week. Anyone is invited, but some of the kids are in foster homes."

"Wow." She only wished she'd had a safe place to go when she was a teen. "That's a good idea."

He smiled at her comment. "They need someone to talk to at times. They come with their guardians or foster parents, but we team each kid up with a mentor. Supervised, of course."

"That's good. That they're able to talk to someone and that it's supervised."

He went quiet for a couple of moments. "Listen, if you don't want to go—"

He was talking about kayaking, but he must have seen the darkness in her eyes. Pushing aside the flare of distant painful memories, she gave him a weak smile.

"Let me get inside and change," she said, making a snap decision she hoped she wouldn't regret. "I haven't been kayaking in a while so I might slow you down, but yes, I'd like to take a ride around the lake."

"Good. I'll go get the kayaks ready. You can meet me at the boat landing."

"Okay." Vanessa hurried into the house, her mind buzzing with good and bad thoughts. She didn't want to group Rory in the same category as her mother's ex-husband, but how could she not think about it? She'd been a troubled teen, and her so-called stepfather had pretended to be her mentor.

And yet he'd betrayed her in the worst way.

Would Rory do that?

No. Because for one thing, Vanessa was a grown woman now. Stronger and more assertive. No longer afraid to stand up to people.

Rory Sanderson wasn't anything like Gregory Pardue. Not at all. Thank goodness.

And yet when she came back outside, Vanessa felt a shiver moving down her spine. Was she making a mistake, getting to know the preacher?

She looked up at the sky and for the first time in years, she asked God to protect her heart. Because she didn't want to be wrong about Rory.

Chapter Six

She'd found a pair of old cutoff jeans and rolled them up over her knees. A sleeveless cotton blouse covered the shorts. Swallowing her trepidations, Vanessa walked the short distance to the lake's boat landing near the marina and boardwalk. The sun felt good on her skin, and the sound of seagulls flying overhead reminded her that summer was coming.

She saw Rory waiting with the two kayaks. He waved and she waved back. He had on shorts and an old T-shirt. He was much darker than her, which showed he got outside more than she did.

Not the pasty-skinned pallor she considered more minister type. But then, Rory shattered all of her notions regarding preachers. He looked as if he belonged on a California beach instead of here, standing by two kayaks and waiting on her.

"You ready for this?" he asked, sincerity in his blue eyes.

"Yes. I'll probably regret it tomorrow—sore muscles— but I need to get out and get some exercise. Moving boxes and going through closets and cabinets doesn't count as a fun way to get in shape."

He gave her a quick once-over. "You know how to kayak, right?"

She thought she remembered. "Yes. Love it."

He motioned her to where he had the kayaks pulled up in the shallow water by the concrete landing. "We can do this at the dock or I'll hold yours while you get in."

"I can get in here," she said, glancing around to make sure no one would see her if she fell headfirst into the shallow water. "Or at least I'm going to try."

Rory took her hand while he held the bright blue kayak steady with his foot. "Okay, sit and turn."

Vanessa tried to ignore the warmth of his fingers holding hers. He had a strong, secure grip. "Like a lady getting into a car," she said on a nervous laugh.

"Sorta." He grinned and held on to her while she plopped down into the low, narrow watercraft. "See, you're in."

"Yes, now I have to get my legs in, too." She turned forward, her water shoes intact.

Once she was settled, he handed her the paddle. Vanessa wondered how he'd manage getting inside his red kayak, but he slid in with the ease of someone who was a born athlete. She noticed his muscular arms and broad shoulders. What else would she notice about this man?

Too many things, she decided.

As they glided out onto the lake, Vanessa worked to keep up with Rory, having no doubt that he was purposely going slow to stay with her. But they laughed and talked as they paddled around the big oval body of water. The ducks and geese squawked and fussed as they glided by. People waved from the shore, some of them calling out to Rory.

Spring was in full bloom, showing off in the dappled sunlight. Azaleas lush with pink-and-white flowers clustered underneath the tall pines and old oaks. Crape myrtles along the streets were bursting with tiny blossoms that were beginning to bud in hot pink and deep purple. The old magnolias hung heavy with huge white petals. The green fronds on tall palms danced in the wind, the sound of their frenzy sending out a steady swish, swish. The whole lake smelled like a fragrant, earthy garden.

With the wind in her face and the sun warm on her skin, Vanessa relaxed and remembered the short time she'd spent here in Millbrook Lake so many years ago. Her last couple of years of high school had been spent here. Marla had been one of her friends back then.

Marla was trying to be a friend to her now.

And so was Rory.

"How you doing?" he asked as he paddled close.

"Fine." She held her oar still and smiled over at him. "This is really nice."

Nice. That small word, usually so boring, was fast becoming her favorite expression.

"Anytime you want to go for a spin, let me know," he said, his eyes bright with expectation.

Vanessa nodded and wished she could feel that same hope. But she'd given up on hoping or expecting a long time ago. The best she could manage was a day-to-day positive feeling that involved her work. She'd learned to take care of herself since she'd left Millbrook Lake, and that accomplishment kept her going. Her life involved salvaging vintage clothes and items and reselling them to like-minded people. Which was odd, considering how long she'd been running from her past.

Or maybe she clung to old things so she could hang on to the little bit of good in her past. No matter. She knew what would be in her future. She'd be alone. By choice.

She couldn't risk messing things up with someone the way her mother had. Over and over.

Clearing those cobwebs out of her head, she gave Rory a quick nod. "Thanks. I won't have much time, but I need to remember what a special place this is. The lake and the town—it's all like a picture book."

He drifted closer. "Oh, it looks pretty but we're all living our lives, day by day. Reality can set in at any time. But I can't complain."

"Are you trying to burst my bubble?" she asked, surprised that he'd made such a pointed observation. Where had Mr. Feel Good gone?

He gave her a perplexed glance. "No, not at all. But you know how it goes. This is a great place to live, no doubt about that. But it's our state of mind that adds those little nuances and warm, fuzzy feelings to our lives."

"Oh, so we're discussing that now, are we?" She started paddling again. "My state of mind is in a constant state of turmoil."

"I didn't mean to imply that," he said, pulling up beside her again. "I was trying to say it had more to do with me than you. I didn't mean for it to sound so corny."

She doubted that. He was usually so happy-go-lucky, even the ducks liked him. "And what could you possibly have to be negative about, Preacher?"

He didn't answer right away. Which made her only want to know everything about him. Finally, he said, "More than you'd realize. But you're right. I know better than to preach to someone who's been through enough already. I'm sorry."

Since she'd never heard a negative tone in his voice before, she glanced over to check on him. He looked dejected and brooding. Different. Definitely human.

"No, I'm sorry," she said. "I'm a little prickly these

days. I know you mean well, and I should appreciate how you aren't trying to gloss over things. This isn't Disneyland, after all. I mean, look what Marla went through after her first husband died. And Alec, coming home with wounds that almost turned him into a recluse. Blain and Rikki were almost killed a few months ago. I really don't have it that bad, after all."

"Neither do I," he said. "Look, I want to get to know you, all preacher talk aside. I don't want to preach to you. I want to…talk to you."

"I like talking," she admitted. "Even when I'm down and grumpy."

"You're grieving. Sometimes being still and listening is the best thing for that."

"Now that is good advice," she said with a wry smile. "Truce?"

"Truce," he said. "I need to listen to my own advice."

"Race you to the other side of the lake," she said, taking off in a whirl of paddles and water. Trying to get away from the intimacy of their conversation, too.

Soon they were laughing and calling out to each other. Relieved that they'd gotten past that sticky moment, Vanessa still wondered when this sweet man had been through any kind of turmoil.

They turned back toward the landing just as the sun began to set behind the tree line. Rory hopped out first and tried to help her, but she was up and dragging her kayak close to the shore before he could make a move. When she slipped and almost went down in the muddy shallows, he took her by both hands and lifted her up, his hands moving to her elbows to steady her.

Their eyes met as she came face-to-face with him.

"Thanks," Vanessa said, her breath leaving her body. It had been a long time since she'd felt such a buzz of awareness with a man. And their conversation out there on the lake had only added to that feeling. Something about that little dent in his armor had endeared Rory to her.

"You're welcome." His eyes went a deep sky blue, showing her his awareness of the ripple moving over them like a current. "As I said, anytime."

"I… I'd better get home," she said, pulling away to steady herself. "I've still got lots to do."

Rory tugged the kayaks away from the landing. "Okay."

"Do you need help? I can carry one of these."

"No. I can't make you carry these heavy things."

"I don't mind." She flexed her arms. "I'm not help-less, you know."

He swept her with an appreciative look. "Yes, I've no-ticed that, but I've got it." Then, he grinned. "I enjoyed having someone to tour the lake with. And to talk to."

"Me, too." She turned to go, feeling as if she'd done something wrong. Her abrupt nature could scare any-one away.

"Hey?"

She whirled. "Yes?"

"You're welcome to come to Youth Night if you'd like. I can always use volunteers, especially female volunteers. We get a lot of girls in, and they don't want to open up to a male minister." He shrugged. "It's a tough gig, but we're always looking for mentors."

Vanessa's heart started racing. She felt even more winded than she had after kayaking around the lake. "I… I'll have to think about that and let you know. I'm not sure I'll be here long enough to get involved."

"Okay. But even attending a few meetings can make a world of difference for someone." He gave her one of his dazzling grins. "We order pizza and sometimes watch movies."

"Sounds like fun." Or something she couldn't deal with.

After thanking him again, she escaped to the darkness of the house, shutting the door and leaning back against it. Closing her eyes, Vanessa wished she'd had a better answer than a stumbling, halting maybe. Could she be any more obvious?

But being around troubled teens? Did she want to live through that kind of turmoil again? Even if she wasn't the one going through it?

She'd have to really think hard on how to handle that request. With each invitation, Rory was also drawing her in more and more.

In spite of that, she liked him. A lot. But she did not like the idea of getting involved in church. At all.

"What should I do?" she asked the darkness. "What should I do?" she asked God.

She remembered when she'd been alone and frightened, with no one to talk to because she was so afraid no one would believe her. Her own mother hadn't believed her, so why would anyone else?

What if one girl out there needed a friend, someone she could trust?

It doesn't have to be me.

But why shouldn't it be you?

Going to the refrigerator, she found a bottle of water and opened it and took a long drink. Why not her? What else did she have to do besides go through this sad, cluttered house and then leave town once it was sold?

No commitment. Just a helping hand.

She could do this. She needed to do this.

Even if she'd vowed never to have children of her

own, she might be able to help a teenager at least. Now she'd have to find the courage to take those few steps to the church doors.

Rory checked the snack table. Mr. and Mrs. Peppermon had outdone themselves tonight. The couple fostered two of the teens who attended Youth Night, and they always insisted on helping with the food, too. In spite of their tight budget and dealing with their grandchildren's busy schedules, they loved helping out at the church. Devoted. They were devoted.

Rory thanked the Lord for that.

"Hello."

He turned to find Miss Fanny ambling into the small gathering room at the back of the church. "Hey, there. What are you doing here?"

"I was in the neighborhood," she said, coy. "I made some oatmeal cookies, and I can't possibly eat all of them. Thought the kids might enjoy them."

Rory gave her a hug. "Of course they'll love your cookies. And you can visit with them and have dinner with us since you *live* in the neighborhood."

"I'd like that." She grinned and glanced around. "Is your new friend coming tonight?"

"My new friend?"

"Vanessa. I've tried to catch her coming and going to introduce myself, but she's too quick for me."

"She is a slippery little thing," Rory retorted. "And I did invite her to come. But…she's still a bit gun-shy."

"We can fix that by making her feel better about things."

"Right." Rory thought about how he'd botched that idea out on the lake the other day. He hadn't talked to

Vanessa since. For oh so many reasons. "I think we should let her hang out and see how it goes."

"Okay, I'll mind my own business," Miss Fanny said, her pink hat full of real flowers and plastic Easter eggs. "She won't even know I'm here."

Rory grinned and offered Miss Fanny a chair. "The kids should be arriving soon."

Wanda Peppermon came out of the small church kitchen, carrying a huge casserole dish of lasagna, the spicy scent wafting straight toward Rory's hungry nose.

"Let me help with that," he said, grabbing the pot holders and the dish from her. "You didn't have to cook, you know. We have a hefty pizza budget."

"I know," Wanda said, her salt-and-pepper hair curling against the collar of her blousy shirt. "But Kandi loves homemade lasagna, so I thought this might cheer her up. She's been in a mood all week."

Rory searched the room. "Where is Kandi?"

"Outside, sitting on a bench. She didn't want to come tonight. I think it's got something to do with her mother's birthday. It's this week."

Rory's heart went out to the pretty teen. Her mother died when she was ten and she never knew her daddy, so she'd been forced into the foster program. She'd resented the world for a long time now.

"Should I go and talk to her?" Rory asked Wanda.

"Let her sit a while," Wanda said. "She'll be in when the others start coming. She has her eye on a boy she met in school, and I'm not so sure that's a good idea. He's not exactly a good influence, so we've been keeping an eye on that situation."

Rory nodded. "Okay. We'll give her some space. I'll go help Carl with the cups and ice."

Wanda chuckled. "Check on my husband's choice of

drinks, too. He got sugary soda when I told him to get lemonade."

"We can have both," Rory said. "I have big cans of powdered lemonade."

Rory glanced around one more time when he heard the door to the sunny gathering hall opening. Would Vanessa show up?

Chapter Seven

Vanessa stood on the front steps of her house, casting covert glances over at the church. She'd been standing there at least ten minutes, watching as a few adults and several teenagers trickled into the church gathering room.

She should go on over there and get it over with. She'd gone by Marla's Marvelous Desserts and bought two dozen cupcakes, and she sure couldn't eat them all by herself.

Well, actually she could do that. But she shouldn't. She wouldn't. Unless tonight went badly, and then she'd bring them back home and eat at least three. But she'd promised Marla she would make an effort.

"Oh, please do," Marla had said, all cheery and smiling. "Rory tries so hard, and a lot of these kids need the affirmation of good adult friends. You'll be perfect, Vanessa."

Not so perfect but she was interested.

Steeling herself, she grabbed the cupcake boxes and checked her black jersey flared skirt and floral T-shirt. She'd pass muster since most of the teens were wearing shorts and T-shirts anyway.

Halfway there, she noticed a young girl sitting on the

top of an old picnic table near the curb. The girl looked so dejected and alone, Vanessa's heart went out to her. Maybe she'd come inside and Vanessa could meet her. But what would they talk about? The weather? The latest movies?

Vanessa felt out of her element. How could she even think she might be able to be some sort of mentor to a troubled teen? She'd be leaving soon and besides, she avoided children like the plague.

As she neared the church, the girl glanced up and right into Vanessa's eyes with a daring stare full of attitude. She had short brown spiked hair and wore a torn bright blue T-shirt over baggy black pants, the dark kohl around her eyes matching her even blacker lace-up boots. Bangles and string bracelets of every shape and color folded against each other like an accordion up and down both her wrists. And a big clunky necklace full of various charms weighed down her neck like an albatross.

Immediately intrigued, Vanessa smiled. "Hi," she said as she neared the girl.

The girl kept staring but didn't say anything.

Vanessa tried again. "I…uh… I love your jewelry. Eclectic."

A distrustful stare followed by surprise and a mumbled, "Thanks."

"Are you going inside?"

"I'm waiting for someone."

"I'm new here," Vanessa said, her heart hurting for this girl. She looked forlorn and lost, and her attitude was too familiar. "I kind of dread going in there."

The girl gave her another bored glance. "Why?"

"I don't like being part of organized religion."

A snort followed by another baffled stare. "Then why are you here?"

Vanessa moved a couple of feet closer. "I don't know, really. It's just that—"

A tall, lanky boy with jet-black hair walked up behind the girl and put his arms around her waist. Giving Vanessa a sullen glance, he said, "Hey, baby," into the girl's triple-pierced ear.

"Rocky," the girl said with a real smile that made her beautiful. "I thought you'd ditched me."

"Never. But you could ditch this stupid place and come with me."

The girl shot Vanessa a glance—part tell-me-stay and part don't-you-dare-stop-me.

Vanessa saw trouble all over this. "Hey, let's get inside before all the food is gone."

The girl glanced back at Romeo-Dracula and then gave Vanessa a strange glaring look. "I have to go inside, Rocky. My foster mom won't let me leave with you. So if you don't want to stay, I guess we can't do anything together after all."

Rocky shot Vanessa an accusing stare full of blame. "So, don't ask her. This nice lady won't tell, will you?"

Vanessa stepped closer. "I don't want to sound bossy, but you really should come inside with me. You're right. Your foster mother will be worried."

"Hey, lady, back off," Tall, Dark and Pale said, his winged eyebrows reminding Vanessa of a skinny bat.

The girl whirled on him. "She's trying to be nice."

"Nice?" The boy stepped away as if he'd been burned. "Nice? Is that seriously a word?"

"It is if you know how to use your manners," the girl said. "Which you obviously don't."

"Whatever!"

The boy gave Vanessa a rage-filled glare and turned to stalk away. The girl hopped off the bench and almost went after him. But she pivoted instead, her face full of a jagged resolve. "Well, that didn't last very long."

"I'm sorry," Vanessa said. "I shouldn't have interfered."

But she was glad she had.

The girl brushed past her with more than a dollop of swagger. "I was gonna break up with him anyway."

Vanessa wanted to say something else when she looked up to find Rory standing outside the gathering hall doors, a surprised grin on his handsome face.

"How much of that did you hear?" Vanessa asked Rory after Kandi whirled past him with her gaze on her boots.

"Enough," he said, wondering why Vanessa and Kandi had been talking in the first place. "Did she say something smart-alecky to you?"

"No. We were beginning to have a conversation when some sort of Goth James Dean tried to entice her to go away with him."

Rory took in Vanessa's pretty outfit and the white boxes marked with Marla's trademark dessert label. "So…you stopped Kandi from making a really bad mistake?"

"I suggested we should go inside, yes."

"Good move. Wanda, her foster mother, told me Kandi has been hanging out with a boy who might not be suitable. So where is Mr. Wonderful?"

"He got mad and swooped away after Kandi basically told him to get some manners."

"Good for her." Rory took the pastry boxes. "You brought goodies."

"I wasn't sure what to bring," Vanessa said, looking as if she'd like to run back home. "I wasn't sure if I'd even come."

"I know." He leaned close. "You can leave at any time. We have several exit doors."

She gave him one of her half smiles. "Thanks." Then she glanced toward the door to the building. "So that girl, Kandi, is in the foster program?"

"Yes. She just turned sixteen. Lost her mother when she was ten and never knew her father. The Peppermons have had her for about six months now. She's a handful but she's been through a lot. She's been better lately, but her mom's birthday is this week. She would have been thirty-two if she'd lived."

Shock registered on Vanessa's face. "She died?"

"In a car wreck. She was drinking and driving. She had Kandi when she was sixteen, so I'm sure the whole thing is weighing on the girl."

The shock changed to understanding. "Oh. That's horrible."

Rory wondered if Vanessa was thinking of her own mother. "Yep. Kandi's acting out because she misses her mother. She has no grandparents who live near. Her mother's parents live in California and don't really want anything to do with her since she gave them so much trouble when they did try to raise her."

They strolled into the long building behind the church. "I can't imagine that," Vanessa said. "Even on our worst days, my mother and I still tried to communicate. Obviously, we never succeeded but still…"

"Maybe you two were closer than you realized."

She glanced around the room full of teens of various sizes and ages. "Maybe so. I guess we'll never know now, will we?"

Then she took the pastry boxes from him and marched toward the food table.

Rory decided Kandi wasn't the only female around here with attitude. But Vanessa had pushed aside her issues to come tonight. It was a start. He followed her and began introducing her to various people.

"I think you met Kandi Jordan outside," he said to Vanessa when they walked by the girl. "Kandi, this is my friend Vanessa Donovan. She lives across the street, but she's only here for a few weeks. She came back to clean out her house and sell it."

Kandi shot Vanessa a sullen glance. "Why are you selling your house?"

Vanessa's eyes grew wide with concern. "My mother died a few weeks ago. I don't want to live here so I have to sell it."

Rory filled in the blanks to keep the awkwardness at bay. "Vanessa loves vintage stuff, and she's agreed to hold her estate sale in conjunction with our rummage sale here at the church. If you volunteer to help out, I'm sure you might find some cool items."

"I don't need anything," Kandi said before turning away to talk to another girl.

But Rory saw the way she sent a kohl-eyed glance back at Vanessa. "I think she's warming up to you," he whispered to Vanessa.

"Right." Vanessa shook her head. "Reminds me of myself at that age."

"I imagine you were cute at that age."

"I was a real pill," she replied. "All gangly legs and messy hair. And braces."

"I wore braces," he said. When he spotted Miss Fanny, he nudged Vanessa toward where the older woman sat holding court. "I want you to meet someone."

Miss Fanny looked up at Rory with a wide smile, and then her gaze moved to Vanessa, her hands going to her mouth.

"Miss Fanny, this is Vanessa. Your neighbor."

"Hello," Vanessa said, her eyes moving from the woman in the chair to Rory, a questioning look in her eyes. "It's nice to meet you."

"You look like your mama," Miss Fanny said. "She was a pretty woman."

"You knew my mother?" Vanessa asked, her words caught on a breath of surprise. She sent Rory another glance, this one with a tad of accusation coloring it. He didn't remind her that he'd mentioned this to her.

"I sure did," Miss Fanny said before Vanessa could argue the point. "We were good friends back in the day. Artists, you know. Sensitive and so sure we could save the world with words and colors. I live right next to your house. I wish I could talk to her over the fence one more time."

Vanessa's eyes went misty. "Me, too." Then she gave Rory an expression full of pain. "It's good to see you. I...I think I need to find the ladies' room."

"Down the hallway," Miss Fanny said, pointing. After Vanessa hurried away, she lifted her eyes to Rory. "I didn't mean to upset her."

"She's still grieving," Rory explained. "In more ways than one."

"Grief never really goes away," Miss Fanny said, eyeing the hallway. "I could go and check on her."

"I think she'd rather be alone right now," Rory said. "I'll send someone in if she's not out soon." He checked his watch. "I need to bless the food so we can get started."

But he took one more glance toward the ladies' room. Would Vanessa come out, or would she sneak out the back door and go home?

She should go home.

Vanessa blew her nose and stared at herself in the mirror, her gaze moving over the fresh flowers on the van-

ity and the picture of a mother and child walking along
the lake centered on the wall over an inviting wooden
bench. When she heard someone coming in, she threw
the tissue in the trash and pushed at her hair.

Kandi stood behind her with big eyes wide with questions. "So...your mother died?"

Vanessa put on a brave face. "Yes. She'd been sick
for a while."

"My mom died in a bad wreck. Her birthday is Friday."

Vanessa turned to face the girl and noticed her vivid
green eyes. "I'm so sorry to hear that."

"I was young," Kandi said. She shrugged and leaned
over the counter, her black polished nails raking through
the tufts of spiky hair around her face. "I don't really remember much about her."

Right. A ten-year-old would remember a lot of things.

Vanessa figured Kandi remembered way more than
she needed to. "Do you have pictures of her? Things that
might help you remember?"

Another shrug and then a swipe at dark red lips. "I
have two pictures. I'm in one. And I have some clothes
and stuff. I move around a lot, so I don't have much of
anything."

"The Peppermons seem nice," Vanessa said, not wanting to upset the girl.

"Nice." Kandi actually cracked a smile. "There's that
word again."

"Yep." Vanessa smiled right back, remembering how
that seemed to be her new word. "Let's change it to special, understanding, sweet, tolerant—"

"Fun, playful, determined, demanding, fair," Kandi
finished. "I like them. I didn't like some of the others."

A dark shadow passed over the girl's eyes. A shadow

that Vanessa recognized immediately. But before she could ask Kandi if anything had happened to her in one of the other homes, a woman poked her head inside the door.

"Preacher wanted me to check on you two and tell you supper is served."

"We'll be right out," Vanessa said. "Ready, Kandi?"

The girl nodded and brushed past the woman at the door. "As ready as I'll ever be."

Vanessa and the woman exchanged knowing glances. "I know that feeling," she said with a smile.

The woman grinned. "Me, too." Then she gave Vanessa a big smile. "I'm Barbara, by the way. I'm the church secretary."

"Nice to meet you," Vanessa said. She cringed inwardly. That word *nice* was being overused today.

When Vanessa came back up the hall, she saw Rory and waved. He walked over to her. "Want to sit with Miss Fanny and me? Or do you want me to walk you home with a to-go plate?"

"I'm staying," she said, her tone firm. "I'm hungry."

"That's a good sign," he said.

But Vanessa wasn't staying for the food. She wanted to get to know Kandi a little better. Because she needed to know if that young girl had suffered the same humiliation that she had.

And if so, she intended to do something about it.

Chapter Eight

Vanessa listened while Rory did his thing. He read a short devotional about accepting God's love and allowing the Lord to love us.

"Sometimes, we think we're not worthy of God's love," he explained. "But if we think that, we're doing the Lord a disservice. He died for our sins. That makes us worthy. We need to honor His sacrifice by accepting His love into our hearts."

And that was it. No shout-outs about sinners. No condemnations about not sitting in church every Sunday. After the devotional, Rory asked some questions and got the kids to talking. He glanced at her a couple of times, his smile so sure and full of life that Vanessa had to swallow back the pain that seemed to clog her throat.

Why couldn't she feel that kind of peace and joy?

Was she worthy?

Or was she being too cynical for her own good?

"What if we don't deserve God's love?"

She glanced around to find a young boy sitting toward the back. Rory nodded at the boy, too.

"Hi, Mark," Rory said. "That's a good question. And the answer is even better. We *don't* really deserve God's love, but we are worthy. That probably doesn't make a lot of sense, but we're worthy only because we are alive and because God's love is unconditional. So that makes all of us worthy in His eyes even if we don't feel worthy."

"I don't get it," Mark said with a shrug. "Why would God want to fool with someone like me?"

"You don't have to actually get it all the time," Rory said. "But stay open to the possibilities. A lot can happen when you're open to love. Good things can happen—to you, to me, to anyone who wants the Lord in their life."

"Not always. Bad things can happen, too."

Kandi.

Vanessa's gaze slammed into Rory's, and she saw the understanding and compassion in his eyes. "You got me there, Kandi," he said. "I've had some bad things happen in my life and…it's not easy. I turned on God, ranted at Him. And then I made some bad choices to prove my point."

"How'd you become a preacher then?" someone else asked.

Rory's gaze locked on Vanessa. "I kind of went into a bad spot, and then I went to war."

Vanessa tried to remain passive. Marla had mentioned Rory had served as an army chaplain, but it sounded as if he'd gone to war to fight. Or maybe to escape?

Kandi lifted her gaze to Vanessa. "Have you had anything bad happen to you, besides your mother dying?"

Still reeling from Rory's candid admission, Vanessa nodded. "Yes. I've been hurt by people. At times I feel as if God has abandoned me." Because she didn't like being pinned to the spot, she shrugged. "But I've managed to take care of myself for a very long time."

"Don't we need God in our lives?" another teen asked,

his eyes wide with hope. "To help us through the tough times?"

"Yes," Rory said. "Yes, we do. But it's hard sometimes to see that. Christ offers us comfort when we feel alone and abandoned, even if we can't understand how it all works."

"I pray," someone else said. "I pray and hope…and I wait."

A petite blonde bobbed her head. "Me, too."

Kandi rolled her eyes and sliced her fingers through her hair, her gaze still on Vanessa. "I'm tired of waiting."

Vanessa certainly knew that feeling. But maybe waiting was all part of the process. Maybe she needed to be still and listen. And wait.

"You went to war," Vanessa whispered to Rory a while later, her gaze full of questions. "Marla mentioned you were a chaplain, but I didn't think of that as being dangerous. I mean, it is dangerous but I didn't understand why you joined up. It sounded as if you were pretty angry about a lot of things."

Rory wasn't ready to talk about this. He rarely talked about his past to anyone. But this was Vanessa. It wouldn't be fair to her that he'd tried so hard to draw her into his world without telling her a little about himself.

"I should have explained it to you."

And he should have explained things when that kid had asked, but he'd managed to get by with a vague response about joining the army and really seeing what life and death were all about. It wasn't enough and it didn't give anyone any answers. Rory didn't have all the answers. Who did?

He needed to tell Vanessa the truth, at least. But not yet. "I had some issues," he said, hoping to leave it at that.

"So you were mad at God?"

"Yep. I was so mad at the world and at God that I up and joined the army. I'd finished seminary, and I thought I was ready to find my first church home and I did. But I kind of messed up things from the get-go."

"Why were you so angry?" she asked, surprise in every word.

Rory guided her toward her house. Everyone else had left, including Miss Fanny. He'd offered to walk Vanessa home and she'd accepted, but only because she obviously wanted him to finish his story.

"That's for another night," he said, not ready to bare his soul. He glanced back toward the church. "I hear you and Kandi plan to meet up at Wanda's house once you're all cleared to become a mentor."

"Yes." She looked uncertain and maybe a little disappointed that he wasn't telling all. "I'm nervous."

"Listening is key when you're a mentor to a troubled teen."

"I don't know if I can do that. What if I mess up?"

"You can't mess up. Wanda will monitor you two and help you out." He shifted on his dock shoes. "But we made progress tonight, don't you think?"

She stopped at the steps to her house. "Oh, you mean, you got me across the street? So now, you'll keep stringing me along with little tidbits of your story so I'll keep coming back?"

"I'm not stringing you along," he said, wondering if she had him pegged. "I have a past, too, Vanessa. And I don't always like to talk about it."

"You?" Her eyes glistened in the moonlight. "You have a past?"

"It happens," he said on a defensive note. "It happens

to most people, you know. We all make mistakes or have bad times."

"But you, not you." She sat down on the porch steps. "You're so…well…nice." She groaned. "I've used that word way too much tonight, but it fits with you."

"Sometimes nice guys make bad mistakes," he said. "Nice can cover a multitude of sins."

She looked surprised. "Can you tell me a little about what happened and why?"

Rory took that as an invitation and sat down next to her. "Why me?" He gazed out at the moonlight hitting the lake in a gray-white shimmer. "I can tell you this much. I…was an orphan."

"What?" She twisted to stare over at him. "You were a foster kid?"

"Yes." He gave her one quick glance and then turned back toward the night. "I bounced around a lot but when I was twelve years old I came here to live with a wonderful couple who decided to adopt me. We moved to Crestview when I was a teenager. But I didn't stay there, obviously. I left right after I graduated high school."

"Where did you go after that?"

"I got a job and paid my way through college." He stopped and took a breath. "I went to seminary and set out to be a minister but… I had a few setbacks. I was angry and confused, so I wound up joining the army."

He hadn't talked about that part of his life in a long time. His buddies knew he was adopted and that he'd served as a chaplain, but they didn't even know all of the details about his adult life and they didn't ask. They knew Rory would talk about it when he was ready.

But could he ever be ready?

Vanessa sat staring at him. "You decided to join the

army because you were angry? Were you angry because you were a foster kid?"

"Yes," he said. It had started there. He still didn't know who his real parents were. "I guess I was angry for most of my life, even after I was placed with good parents. I was abandoned as a baby. And my adopted father died when I was a teenager. My mother is still alive, thankfully. She still lives in Crestview."

Vanessa didn't speak for a couple of moments. "Wow."

"Yep, wow."

"I'm sorry. I mean, that's tough."

"Tough comes in all kinds of ways, to all kinds of people."

"But that really *is* tough."

"I got over it."

"You are full of revelations, Preacher."

"Yep. We all are." He wanted to hear her revelations.

"So is that why you started this youth program?"

"One of the reasons. I want to help them, give them hope before they do something stupid. I understand how they feel."

"I do, too," she said, her tone quiet. "I'd like to get to know Kandi a little more. What should I do besides visit with her and Wanda?"

Happy that she'd decided that, Rory turned to Vanessa. "I'm sure Wanda told you there are rules, of course, to protect the children. You'd be vetted and you can't be alone with her, so that's why you have to meet her with Wanda nearby, probably at their house and at the church, of course. We get together each week, and each mentor sits with their teen. Let her talk without judging her and respond as a friend, as someone who cares."

"Okay. I… I'm not good with children. I don't know if I'll ever have any of my own."

Rory muzzled his surprise with a laugh. "I don't think anyone feels they're good with children until they actually have children."

"And sometimes, they're not good then either," she said on a quiet whisper.

Before he could respond, she pushed to stand. "I should get inside."

Rory stood, too, and placed his hand on her elbow to steady her. "And I should get back to the church. I have to check everything and lock up."

Their eyes met, the moonlight playing over them like a diffused spotlight. Rory saw so much in her gaze, but he also saw the hidden things. "I'm glad you came," he said, his throat going raw with a huskiness that seemed too intimate.

"Me, too." She didn't move to go inside. She kept her eyes on him. "I hope Kandi will let me get to know her."

"We'll try it," he said, stepping back. "I'll help you with her. She's a special girl, and she could use a friend."

Vanessa nodded and looked out at the lake. "I guess we could all use a friend at times." Then she smiled at him. "I hope one day, you'll tell me the rest of your story, Rory."

Rory wanted to hug her close. This was crazy. Feelings he'd long buried swirled and resurfaced in a different current, in a new pattern. But this time, with a different woman. A woman who didn't want children. A woman who might not want anyone.

But she needed someone. And she needed to believe in herself, too.

Suddenly, Rory couldn't breathe, couldn't decide whether to run away or move closer. He'd vowed never to fall in love again. It hurt too much.

He'd only planned to minister to this woman.

Now he also wanted to kiss this woman.

"Vanessa," he said, about to explain why he couldn't do this, why he wasn't ready for this.

"I have to go," she said, moving up the steps.

"Me, too." He stepped down to the walkway. "I'll see you…later."

She turned at the door. "Yes, later."

And then she was inside. Out of his reach.

Rory took his time getting back to the church. He had some serious praying to do. But he wasn't sure how to pray. Did he ask God to bring him closer to Vanessa? Did he ask in a spiritual way? Or did he plain out ask God to help him in a romantic way?

Was he finally ready to love again?

The next day, Vanessa stared at her mother's cluttered bedroom. In the early-morning light, it looked even worse. Gaudy and tarnished, dusty and dirty. Sad. When had Cora gone from being an artist to becoming a hoarder?

Maybe after you left?

But her mother had been happy with Richard. That marriage had worked out for the better. Richard Tucker was a decent, loving man. He'd spent his time divided between this home and the big house in Birmingham, and her mother had traveled with him. But he'd also been a busy man who owned several vast properties and businesses. Had Cora felt lonely and neglected? She must have been lonely after Richard died.

Vanessa remembered arguing with her mother, trying to make her see that Gregory Pardue had been a bad man. Cora wouldn't hear any of it.

"I don't believe you. You're angry that we moved here. You ran him off, you know. Your lies forced Gregory to leave me."

"I'm getting away from here," Vanessa had screamed. "As soon as I can."

A few weeks later, her mother was back out there, trolling for another husband. And she'd found Richard Tucker. Richard had calmed both of them.

Vanessa had attended his funeral in Birmingham, but she hadn't stayed around to help her mother with anything. Selfish? Or part of Vanessa's need for self-preservation?

She should have stayed a few days longer, but Cora had a way of starting in on people that soon turned to playing a blame game. Vanessa blamed herself enough without having to hear it from someone else.

Her mother had always been needy.

And Vanessa had fought hard never to need anyone.

"Time to get this over with," she said to the dust balls floating all around her. And to the guilt hovering on her shoulders. She'd avoided this room. Keeping the door to the other bedroom closed had been easy. That room had been Vanessa's. She didn't sleep there. She'd been sleeping on the couch in the den and sometimes on the rattan sofa out in the enclosed sunroom on the far side of the house.

But she couldn't put this off any longer. She'd have to clean all of the bedrooms, starting with her mother's and working her way through the small room her mother had used mostly for storage and more collectibles. And then, what had once been Vanessa's room.

Deciding to start with one corner of the big master bedroom, she planned to work her way around the perimeter. The dresser begged to be rescued from the weight of too many paperbacks and old newspapers. No telling what she'd find, but it would be good to have one clean surface.

After dragging a trash can over by the window, Vanessa opened the drapes wide and then pried the window up to let in some fresh air. Then she leaned against the windowsill and thought about Rory.

Why did he tug at her heartstrings so much?

Vanessa went over her usual checklist for men.

Kind. Cute. Steady income. Respectful to women and children. Good with animals. Hardworking and compassionate.

Rory fit the bill more than anyone else she'd ever come close to dating.

But he couldn't. He shouldn't. He was a preacher. So not her type at all. Plus, she hadn't come here to date anyone. She couldn't consider Rory as anything but a friend.

And what do you have to base that on besides an older man who had his own agenda?

Rory had secrets. Now that he'd admitted that to her, Vanessa had one very good reason to avoid him. She didn't like secrets. She'd carried hers long enough to know how they could fester and destroy anything good.

But he's different. Rory is a good person.

Vanessa turned away from the window and the view of the quaint church across the street. She'd never even noticed that church when she'd lived here. Nor did she remember Miss Fanny from next door. Probably because she had been so self-absorbed and so intent on making her mother miserable that she didn't have room in her heart for anything else.

"I'm paying for that now," she said into the morning breeze. "And I'm praying about it, too. In case anyone is listening up there."

Determination made her start digging through the rubble of this room. After about an hour of tossing magazines and sorting through clippings of projects her mother had never started, her hand hit on a leather-bound book. Dusty and worn, it looked like a notebook.

She turned it over and saw a lock on it.

A journal?

Her mother's journal?

She held it close, wondering if she should throw it away without trying to read it or if she should tear it open and find a quiet spot to pore over the whole thing.

When she heard a knock at the door, she jumped and tossed the journal onto the old faded-blue chenille bedspread. Thinking she should ignore the knock, Vanessa checked her hair in case it was Rory.

She looked like she'd just woken up, all smudged and unkempt. Well, he'd get to see the real Vanessa.

But it wasn't Rory standing at her door.

The older woman she'd met last night stood there, leaning on a cane, her big floppy straw hat covered with tiny plastic daisies. "Hello, Vanessa. Remember me? I live next door."

"Miss Fanny, right?" Vanessa asked, surprised to see the woman. "How are you?"

"I'm good, darlin'. I baked you some braided bread. It's mighty good with butter and jam for breakfast."

"Oh, how nice." Vanessa took the foil-wrapped bread. It was still warm, the scent tickling at her nose. "It sure smells good."

"I can assure you, it is good. I've been baking that bread for over forty years. My husband, Herbert, liked it with lasagna."

Vanessa's stomach growled in glee. "I haven't had breakfast. Maybe I'll just have a nibble." She gave Miss Fanny a smile and waited for the woman to leave.

Which she didn't.

"Do you have any tea?" Miss Fanny asked. "I have

a hankering to sit out in the garden and drink some hot tea. You could join me, and we could slice up that bread."

Vanessa couldn't say no. Miss Fanny had brought her food…and this woman had known her mother. Maybe they could compare notes. "You know, I've been going through my mother's bedroom, clearing out the junk, and I need a break. We could sit out in the sunporch. I have the windows open, and it's nice and shady. If you'd like to come inside, I'll make the tea and slice the bread."

"I'd love that," Miss Fanny said. "I know my way to the porch, suga'. Your mother and I used to sit out there a lot."

Vanessa held the door while Miss Fanny took her time moving inside. Then she led the way to the back of the house. The French doors to the sunporch were open. "I did clean the porch the other day. I like it out here."

"I'll find a chair and wait for you," Miss Fanny said, her gaze settling on the pillow and blanket on the sofa. "We have a lot to talk about."

Vanessa glanced toward the bedroom where the journal lay on the big bed. She itched to read that journal. But maybe she did need to wait a while.

She had little time to spare, but talking to someone who might actually shed some light on her mother's strange but colorful life could be a step toward forgiveness and understanding. And besides, Miss Fanny was safe and comfortable and easy to talk to.

Not like the preacher across the street. He was easy to talk to, of course. Too easy. Too tempting. But he deserved someone special in his life. A woman who'd be willing to help him serve the people he loved.

Vanessa needed to get to know a few more people while she was here. Just for variety. And for her sanity.

Because having bread and tea with a lonely but considerate old woman had to be safer than standing in the moonlight with Rory Sanderson.

Chapter Nine

The weekend stretched out before Vanessa like a welcoming beach blanket. The sun was shining and the humidity was low for a change. Spring popped out on every corner and in every color, bringing the fragrances of a thousand blossoms wafting out over the warm breeze.

Standing at one of the open windows, Vanessa inhaled the scents of jasmine, honeysuckle and gardenias. Her mother had always loved gardenias. When Richard had heard Cora talking about the sweet-smelling plants, he'd ordered several from the local nursery and had them planted by both the front and back doors.

"When you sit on either of the porches, darlin'," he'd told Cora in his cultured Alabama voice, "you'll be able to enjoy your gardenias."

Why couldn't Richard have come into their lives earlier? Vanessa thought how different things might have been. Stability, love, hope, contentment, joy. All of those things could have been theirs. But instead, Vanessa had been pulled from pillar to post, and Cora had been used and abused by men who didn't care about or respect women.

Not even when one of those men had been a so-called minister.

Turning from the window, Vanessa stared at the racks full of clothes and the card tables covered with knick-knacks she planned to display at the estate sale.

Making a mental note to check one last time with the newspaper about the ad, Vanessa walked through the house again. So much left to throw out, give away or sell. But she had found some gems.

Gorgeous retro dresses from the sixties and seventies and beautiful pieces of costume jewelry, several shelves of books and cabinets full of old china and valuable ceramics.

Her mother had collected odds and ends for her art, but she'd also collected designer shoes and handbags and exquisite Hull vases and Roseville pottery. Each husband or boyfriend had bought Cora things, hoping to make her love them.

Cora had loved Richard. But Vanessa had to wonder if he hadn't died a few years after they'd gotten married, would Cora have turned on him, too?

This house was a gold mine.

But Vanessa figured the real jewel would be her mother's journal. She'd only found the one. Could there be more, hidden somewhere else? Would she find out anything about her absent father in there?

I'm too afraid to read it.

She shook her head, hoping to get back on track. She'd learned not to ask Cora about her father, so why start wondering now? She had too much to do.

Vanessa would keep some of the items and sell the rest on Vanessa's Vintage. She'd already taken photos and cataloged those and put them up on the site. Those items would be shipped to buyers or to the small warehouse she rented in New Orleans. She could sell the jewelry and clothes in her boutique, but she'd wait until after the estate sale to see how much was left.

She'd read that journal when she was done here. Somehow, she couldn't bring herself to do so until she'd cleared up this house. But with each room, a new revelation came. She'd found some of her mother's artwork tucked away in a big closet.

Cora had been a talented artist. Her mother had created whimsical pieces out of mixed media. Big metal flowers stuffed with bits of fabric and button faces. Pretty picture frames made from old jewelry and exotic materials. Purses and hats covered with feathers and flowers. She'd have to save a couple of those for Miss Fanny. Their talk yesterday had helped put some of the pieces together.

"Your mother was a good person, honey. She stumbled a bit."

Vanessa could certainly vouch for that. "I wish I could have really known her," she told Miss Fanny. "The way you did. I watched her work, of course, but she didn't share her artistic side with me very much."

"She didn't share that with anyone," Miss Fanny said. "I had to force her to share with me. She was afraid someone would steal her ideas."

"She always was possessive." Of her art and her men. But not her only child. Cora would shut herself away in the old garage out back—her studio. Even now, Vanessa expected her mother to bark, "Go away, I'm working," when she entered the doors.

Miss Fanny took a sip of tea. "She had a jealous streak."

Miss Fanny told Vanessa stories of their time together, which happened mostly during the hours when Vanessa was at school. Sweet stories that showed a side of Cora

that Vanessa had never noticed. They went to the beach together and shopped and ate meals together. Miss Fanny's
husband tolerated these outings since he was a professor
and was always buried in a textbook. And Miss Fanny
tolerated Cora's mood swings and constant self-doubts.

"We were back and forth across the yards. We'd go to
art fairs and sit all day, hoping to sell one or two pieces.
It wasn't a profitable life, but it was a good life. Your
mother gained some notoriety as a local artist. After she
married Richard, she was happy here until—"

"Until I left and then Richard died."

"Yes. She missed both of you terribly."

They'd talked a bit more before Miss Fanny went back
home. But so much had been left unsaid. Vanessa wondered if her neighbor knew the truth, knew everything.
Didn't good friends share such things? Had Cora walked
across to the little white chapel and asked God to forgive her?

The phone rang, jarring Vanessa away from the dark
memories.

"Hi, it's Marla. How's the sorting going?"

"Slow," Vanessa said. "How are you?"

"Busy," Marla replied. "A lot of birthday parties and
anniversaries. Everyone wants cupcakes or a big cake.
And graduations and Mother's Day are coming up. Busy
blessed."

"You are blessed," Vanessa replied. "I'm preparing for
the big sale and shipping things out for my online site."

"Need any help?"

"No. It's easier to take my time and do it by myself."

"Well, you also need a break. We're having a cookout
Saturday. Want to come over?"

Vanessa glanced at the things still left undone. "That's
tempting. A lot of people?"

"No. Just a few."

Would Rory be there?

She couldn't keep doing this. "I don't know—"

"Yes, Rory will be there," Marla said, her intuitive nature shining through. "Is that a deal breaker?"

"I'm not sure. I mean, he's nice and interesting and... kind."

"But?"

"But I...I want to get this over with and go back to my life."

And she needed to run away from Rory. She would only make him miserable.

"Is it that hard, going through her things?"

"Yes. And no. It's soothing in one way but horrible in another. I found her journal."

"Wow. Did you read it?"

"Not yet. I'm too chicken."

"It's yours now, Vanessa. And it might give you some answers."

"Or it could make things worse."

"You need to hear the good and the bad," Marla said. "Or you'll always wonder."

"I think you're right. I'll read it once I have things in order here."

They talked a few more minutes and then Marla asked, "So, do you want to come over for burgers or not?"

"I'll think about it and let you know. Thanks for inviting me."

She'd put down her phone when the doorbell rang.

Thinking she might not ever get back to work, Vanessa hurried to the door.

And opened it to find Rory standing there.

"Hi," she said, feeling like a guilty kid for having just

talked about him. He wore casual clothes, as usual. A button-up shirt and jeans, dock shoes, no socks.

Again, so different from the image of a minister she held in her memories.

"Hi." He gave her that dazzling smile. "Uh… I was supposed to tell you that we're having a meeting about the rummage sale tonight. Barbara, my adorable and organized barracuda of a secretary, said you need to be there since you'll be having your estate sale at the same time. We'll do flyers to advertise both so people will expect to find both, if you agree. She likes everything neat and tidy with no surprises."

Vanessa had to smile at that. "And you kind of go with the flow, right?"

"Right." He gave her a hopeful stare. "Can you come?"

He looked like a little boy, all grins and excitement.

Contagious.

He was contagious. And she was catching it bad.

"I guess that might be wise. I'll share the cost of the ads. I don't mind paying as a contribution."

"No, oh, no. We take care of such things with an army of stoic volunteers who take their jobs very seriously. Ad cost has been donated already. We might get a healthy competition going between us, though. So be warned."

"You're on," she replied with a smile. She'd give part of her final tally to the church. "What time is the meeting?"

"Six tonight." He glanced behind her. "Hey, you've made progress."

"Yes." She lifted a hand and ignored the warning bell inside her head. "Come in and take a glance."

"Are you sure?"

"Yes." She wasn't sure at all, but she liked being

around him. "I've managed to get through a couple of rooms."

"I can't imagine having to do this. Each item must have a memory."

She nodded. "But they're more her memories than mine. Every now and then I find something that makes me remember more and more, though."

He trailed his fingers over an old leather jacket hanging on a rack. "Do you want to remember?"

"Not all of it, no. But it wasn't all bad. I can see that now."

"I've said it before but I'm offering again. I can help," he said, turning to her. "I want to help."

Vanessa wasn't sure. She couldn't let him in too close to her heart. "You mean, with my memories or this house?"

His eyes went a soft, gentle blue. "With whatever you need."

"Shouldn't you be out nurturing souls or comforting sick people?"

He actually snorted out a chuckle. "Yes, but wouldn't I be doing that by helping you?"

"Do you think I need nurturing or that I'm sick?"

He stepped closer, his blue eyes locking on her. "I think you're grieving and dealing with a lot. You don't have to do it all alone."

"It's getting better," she said, wishing that were true. But pushing him away shielded her from breaking down completely.

He wasn't buying it, however. "Let me help, Vanessa."

Doubt clouded over her need to give in. Anger filtered through the tug and pull of his words. "Why do you want to help?"

"It's what I do. It's how I'm made." He shrugged.

"And besides, I like being with you. Keeps Barbara from badgering me."

"Oh, so you came over here with an excuse about a meeting, but you really want to hide out from your secretary?"

"Yes, something like that."

She knew if she said yes to his offer, this would be a turning point between them. If she said no, he'd go on about his business but he'd keep trying. He *was* made that way.

"Okay," she said, the decision already set. Keeping her tone light, she added, "I do need a big strong man to do some heavy lifting."

"I don't see one of those," he quipped.

"I think you'll do just fine, Preacher."

He winked at her and flexed his muscles.

And Vanessa had to admit, he looked strong and healthy and…good. Too good. She willed herself to a calm she didn't feel. "Let's get started then."

"Lead the way," he said, right behind her.

Too close. But having him close was a new kind of sensation. A pleasant one.

Rory groaned and collapsed on the grass near the open doors of the garage. "Remind me to never, ever ask you if you need help again."

"You did keep after me."

He glanced up at the woman grinning down at him, her fawn-colored hair flowing like a mysterious waterfall around her face. "I did offer, yes."

And he would keep offering. This had gone from trying to get her back right with God to trying to find the courage to ask her out on a date. Could he witness to her over a candlelight dinner?

"I brought iced tea," she said, holding the big plastic cup out over him. Her moods were as swift and unpredictable as the waters out in the Gulf.

A cold drop of condensation hit Rory square on the forehead. "Hey!"

She laughed and backed away. "You might be more comfortable in a chair."

Rory got up and checked his watch. "Okay. A quick drink and then I have to report back, or Barbara will send out a posse."

Vanessa gave him his tea and then took a sip of her own. "I didn't mean to keep you over here so long."

"It's fine. We don't have a lot going on." He shrugged. "Today is sermon day. I'm usually holed up in my office on Thursday afternoon, trying to decide what to say on any given Sunday."

"How *do* you decide what to say?" she asked, her ever-changing hazel eyes shining with questions.

Rory felt that rush of joy he always got whenever someone wanted to know about God. "I pray about it and I search the Scriptures and I follow the calendar—the seasons."

One of her eyebrows lifted while her eyes narrowed. "Ah, the seasons. You mean, like Christmas and Easter?"

"And a whole lot of other seasons," he replied. He could tell her all about that, but now that he'd moved from ministering to possibly making the moves on her, he had to tread very lightly. "Right now it's spring and the flowers are blooming and it's the season of rebirth and new beginnings. Spring always gives me hope."

"Hope?" She looked hopeful. She looked beautiful with the afternoon sun chasing at her.

"Yes, hope. We have to have hope, don't we?"

"I don't know," she said, her smile dimming. "I've forgotten what that's like."

"Well, then, we'll have to remedy that." He stood and drained the sweet, icy tea. "I will see you tonight for the meeting. That's the first order of business."

She followed him to the side gate. "And what's your next order of business after that, Preacher?"

Okay, she was flirting with him.

Now *he* was hopeful. He turned and lifted a finger to her wispy bangs. "That you'll have dinner with me one night soon."

She looked surprised, and then she looked confused. "Are you going to Marla's cookout this weekend?"

"Yes," he said, the one word hinging on so much. "Are you?"

"Yes." She didn't move. "We can let that be a test date."

"A test date? Is there such a thing?"

She turned and tossed a grin over her shoulder. "There is if you're asking *me*."

"Okay," he said, calling after her. "The cookout it is. I love cookouts." And he'd pass the test. He hoped.

"So do I," she shouted back. "I'll see you across the way, Preacher."

"Yes, ma'am."

Rory grinned all the way back to the church.

When he got to the office, he found Barbara standing there, staring up at him with a soft smile. "I think you got lost over there."

"You could say that," he replied. Then he went into his office and closed the door.

Or maybe he got *found*.

Chapter Ten

Well, she'd been in this spot before. Caught between a rock and a hard place, as her mother used to say.

Rory was coming by to walk Vanessa to the cookout. Which was a surprise since he'd been all business at the rummage sale meeting the other night. Nice, polite, full of charm and wit, but he'd also been focused and full of suggestions. He'd glanced at her a couple of times, but always with a shy smile.

He stated their business at the meeting. "So the plan is to open our gathering hall up for the public to come and shop at the Annual Millbrook Lake Church Rummage Sale."

He said this in a booming, official voice, a bit of mirth in his vivid eyes.

"And we'll send our shoppers over to Vanessa's estate sale and encourage them to find some good bargains there, too. Right, Vanessa?"

"Yes. I'll have it all organized and tagged so they can move from room to room. I'm willing to negotiate, too. I have to empty my house and put it up for sale."

Rory had nodded and moved on to other business,

but she'd noticed that bit of regret in his gaze when he'd smiled at her.

Maybe he was being careful since several church members had attended the meeting, too. Not that it mattered. Nothing was going on between them.

But he'd called her early this morning. "Hey, want me to pick you up for the cookout?"

"Uh…it's a block down the street. I thought I'd walk."

"Yes, and I'm coming by to walk with you. I mean, if that's okay."

She almost giggled at the trepidation in his words. Was *that* okay? She'd see him there anyway. "I'd like that. Thanks."

So here she stood, staring in the mirror, wondering if she looked all right. She'd gone way casual, maybe to make a point. A white T-shirt, long jean shorts with rolled cuffs and a colorful scarf draped around her neck. Flip-flops and her hair down around her face. She didn't shout *needy*, but she didn't say *don't look at me* either.

The scarf was her mother's. One she'd found trailing on a closet hook like a clinging vine.

A knock at the door startled Vanessa away from the memories in the mirror. Grabbing the avocado dip she'd made and her phone, she tucked the phone in her pocket and started for the door.

"Hello," she said after opening the door.

The scent of fresh rain greeted her, but it hadn't rained today. Rory had obviously taken a shower since his hair was still damp and curling around his face, and he smelled so clean and outdoorsy she wanted to touch his forehead and play with that sun-streaked hair.

But she'd drop the bowl of dip if she did that.

"Hi," he replied with a smile. "You look great."

Pleased, and annoyed at herself for feeling pleased, she

followed him out the door and made sure it was locked. "Thanks. I worked all day, loaded some pictures on to my site and made calls to some of my vendors, checked on my boutique in New Orleans—"

"Stop! You're making me tired."

She laughed at his mock look of fright. "So what did you do today?"

He glanced out at the lake. A sailboat drifted by like a white bird. "I got up early and went fishing with my friends, and then I came back and went over my sermon for tomorrow and did a little praying and then I took a nap and…now I'm here walking along a beautiful street with a pretty woman. Life is good."

His positive attitude amazed her. She wanted to know more about his life. He must have gone through hard times as a foster child, but now he was so full of life and hope. Contagious, but it was scary. Her heart bumped little beats of warnings coupled with little leaps of joy.

"What's in the bowl?" he asked, taking it from her.

"Hey!"

"I'm trying to be a gentleman. I'll carry it for you."

"It's guacamole dip. I don't cook a lot, but I do make a mean guacamole."

"Sounds good. I'm starving."

"Didn't you eat lunch?"

"Hours ago."

"Poor baby."

He rubbed his flat stomach. "Are we ever gonna get there?"

Vanessa breathed in the scent of jasmine and watched a flock of pelicans flying in a symmetrical line above them. "This is a nice town. I'd forgotten how idyllic it is here."

He let out a contented sigh. "Today is one of those

good days where the humidity got zipped up in a big cloud somewhere on the other side of the world and the sun is clear and the air is crisp." He gave her a sideways glance. "And I'm escorting the prettiest girl on the lake to a picnic. Perfection."

"Do you flirt with all the single ladies in your flock?"

"My flock? What am I, a shepherd?"

"You're with a black sheep."

He looked surprised, his mouth opening to respond. But they had arrived at the open side gate to Alec and Marla's house. "I don't think of you that way," he blurted.

She couldn't help but tease. "You mean, in a flirting way? Or in a black sheep way?"

"Hello!"

Marla's greeting stopped him from replying, but he shot Vanessa a helpless look and gave her a shrug. When she smiled at him, he relaxed a little and followed her into the big backyard.

Marla had gone all out with checked tablecloths and Mason jars full of fresh flowers on each table. An old barrel held iced soft drinks and bottles of water. Up on the deep porch, a long table covered with the same checkered cloths held the side dishes and desserts.

Alec was holding court by a large grill full of burgers, chicken and ribs. He waved. "Hi. Glad you came."

Marla grabbed Vanessa by the arm while Rory went off to talk to Alec. Vanessa noticed a dark-haired man with shaggy hair sitting off to the side, a canned soft drink in front of him on the table. And Gabby's poodle Roxie in his lap. "Who's that?"

"Hunter Lawson," Marla replied. "He's one of the four who own the camp house. But he comes and goes. He got back a few days ago. He's a private investigator now."

"And why is he holding Roxie when he doesn't look like the poodle-dog type?"

"Roxie used to be his—or she belonged to someone he cared about and he inherited her. For a long time, Roxie rode around with him on his motorcycle, but last year he gave her to Gabby. To help Gabby get over her anxieties around strangers. If we go anywhere in a crowd of people, Roxie wears her official service-dog vest."

Vanessa glanced back at the rugged-looking man staring off into space. "He gave Gabby the dog?"

Marla looked over at Vanessa, tears in her eyes. "It was one of the kindest gestures I've ever seen in my life, and I'll be forever thankful to him."

Vanessa didn't know what to say. You never knew about people. What had it cost Hunter to give up the little dog he so obviously loved? What had it cost Rory to serve his country, trying to give people peace in a war-torn world?

Marla checked the food table and turned back toward the kitchen. "I'm going to see about Gabby. She should be waking from her nap soon. Oh, and Blain and Rikki are on their way. Will you watch for them?"

"Sure." Vanessa gained a new respect for the brooding man sitting in the corner. Which only reminded her that she should let go of some of her preconceived notions about people in general. Mainly, preachers in general.

She glanced at Rory and he winked at her.

"He's so cute."

"Yes, he is."

She whirled to find Aunt Hattie standing there with her. "Oh, did I say that out loud?"

Aunt Hattie's smile was serene and sure. "You were mumbling, but I have excellent hearing aids."

"I see." Vanessa busied herself with straightening the

perfectly straight napkins. "I should go and see if Marla needs anything."

"She's fine," Aunt Hattie said. "I tend to leave her to it whenever she's getting together her presentation. After all, she knows what she's doing."

"But you're an amazing cook, too," Vanessa pointed out. "I ate here at Easter, remember?"

"Yes, and Marla and I share the kitchen without any animosity whatsoever," Aunt Hattie replied, a twinkle in her eyes. "But in case you haven't noticed, I'm old and I've done my turn. I don't mind pitching in when needed, but I'm so glad Alec found someone he loves. I couldn't have picked a better person myself. Plus, I love Gabby to pieces. She and I have grand adventures. So I get to kick back and enjoy the happiness around here and help where I'm needed."

"That's not a bad gig." Vanessa loved Aunt Hattie. She was like everyone's fairy godmother.

"And she's needed a lot around here, especially for hugs," Marla said from behind them, pulling Aunt Hattie close.

Gabby giggled and ran past them, her long brown hair flowing around her purple-flowered dress. "Look, Mommy. Uncle Hunter's holding Roxie."

"I see that," Marla called. Then she shook her head and glanced at Vanessa. "She's wide-awake now!" Laughing, she said, "Let's go check on the men."

Vanessa felt a tug of envy and regret as she followed the other women out into the yard. Each time she came here to this old Victorian home, she felt transported to a place she'd never known. A place that shouted home and family. And love. This house looked like a wedding cake and the garden smelled like a perfumery. She thought she could stay in this yard forever.

She glanced at Hunter Lawson. He nodded and went back to staring at nothing, but he did smile when Gabby ran to greet him. Then she remembered that not everyone had such happy endings as this one.

The rest of the afternoon went by quickly. Good food, a lot of small talk, good conversation and a sense of belonging.

Vanessa had enjoyed herself, but her heart ached for something she couldn't seem to see or feel.

"You're deep in thought," Rory said as he slipped up beside her. "Everything okay? We're about to have dessert."

Vanessa couldn't speak. She shouldn't have come here. Now that she'd had a glimpse of this type of happiness, she wanted things she could never have. "I don't know," she said. "I...I think I'm ready to go home."

If she stayed, she'd blurt out her feelings and humiliate herself. Was she being petty and selfish? No. She needed to remember that she had decided long ago to keep her guard up. She couldn't have this kind of life. She was afraid of this. So why was she subjecting herself to this, getting to know a man she couldn't possibly have a relationship with and becoming more and more involved in a world to which she didn't belong?

Rory's concern etched his face in shadows. "Vanessa?"

"I'm tired. I've had a long day, and I guess it finally caught up with me. Would you tell everyone thanks for me?"

She turned and hurried out of the garden.

And she didn't look back.

Rory almost kept walking, but he had to check on Vanessa. After she'd left the cookout, he wanted to go after her, but Marla and Aunt Hattie had cautioned against that.

"She's still dealing with a lot of things," Marla reminded him. "I think seeing all of us here, happy and together, only magnified her pain. I know how she feels. I was like that myself for a long time."

Aunt Hattie had encouraged him to stay for a while. "We'll send a dessert plate with you when you leave. You can check on her then."

So Rory had stayed, and even though the dessert had been as delicious as always, he didn't remember what he'd eaten. He'd counseled a lot of people, but he'd never before gotten so all tied up in wanting to help someone so badly.

Maybe that was part of the problem. He could be too emotionally tied up with Vanessa. He needed to keep a clear head and remember his duty as a minister.

Therefore, he should…walk on by.

But here he was, knocking at the front door.

After several knocks, he decided she didn't want company. Especially not his company. But just as he turned to leave, she opened the door.

"I almost kept going," he said, the foil-wrapped plate in front of him like a shield.

"I almost didn't open the door," she retorted. She had on the same outfit, but her eyes were red and her hair was everywhere.

"Do you want me to go?"

She stared at him, her expression edged with confusion and regret. "Yes. No. I don't know."

"That's not very reassuring, any way you look at it."

"Come in," she said. "I might need that dessert."

"Oh, so I'm just the delivery man?"

"Yes."

He smiled, thinking she was such a paradox. "I hope I get a tip."

She motioned him into the kitchen and pointed toward one of the old chairs tucked underneath a long, plank table. "The best tip I have for you, Preacher, *is* to keep walking."

"Too late for that," he replied. He removed the foil from the plate. "We have some Give Me S'mores Brownies and a couple of cookies. White Chocoholic and Snickerdoodle Oodles, as Marla pointed out..."

She took the plate from him and started nibbling on the brownie, crumbs and marshmallow merging in giant chunks. Rory got up and found her a napkin.

She nodded between chews. "Thanks."

Soon, she was fully engaged with the sweet treats in front of her. "I tend to eat when I'm stressed."

"Don't we all?"

"Food was my comfort growing up," she explained. "When things would go bad, I'd find something to eat. Even though I got my weight under control, kinda, that habit hasn't stopped."

Rory enjoyed watching her, but he wanted to hear about more than her eating habits. "So...why did you bolt?"

She finished the brownie and wiped her hands and face. "Too much beauty," she said in a small voice.

"Excuse me?"

"It was all too much. Everyone so happy and healthy and the house is like the prettiest thing I've ever seen and the yard is this perfect secret garden and I looked at you and it suddenly became too much."

"Do you resent them? Or is this about me?"

"No, I'm happy for them. And yes, this is about you... and me. I've accepted that I'll never have that. I'd made a point of not allowing myself to even think about that type of life—the big house with a garden and kids and dogs running around. I can't see me ever being a mother."

Rory hated the defeat in her words. "Why can't you have all of that?" And what did she mean, telling him this was about him?

And her. Him and her together? Apart? Maybe? Maybe not?

He was beginning to like the *together* idea. Or the *near you* idea, at least.

The image of her sitting in a swing with a child in the backyard of the house she was about to sell hit him somewhere near his solar plexus. Too soon. Way too soon for that kind of daydream. No wonder she'd panicked. He was about to panic, too.

"I've set my standards very low, and I have to get past some issues before I even consider that kind of life."

She was certainly dropping enough hints to give him the picture. She wanted him to back off.

He tried speaking the truth. "Maybe it's too soon after everything you've been through. No one around here expects anything of you, Vanessa. Take time to grieve and to figure out what you need to do for yourself. This isn't about you and me. We're good. We're friends. The rest is up to you."

"Yes, and I should be able to deal with it. I have some good memories, but I'm afraid I brought the bad ones with me because I never cleaned up that part of my life."

Rory could see it now. She'd packed away her emotions, but now that she was being forced to face her past, the clutter was coming out. The clutter and the baggage of a deep pain. "This is not an easy process."

She grabbed one of the cookies. "No. I thought it would be easy but it's hard, Rory. And I want to thank you for being so kind to me." She broke off a chunk of cookie. "I think this is something I have to do on my own. I know I keep telling you that, but it's the only way I can clear my head."

"Is that my cue to leave?"

"No. I need you to understand. You are an amazing man who cares about other human beings, but some things, some people, can't be fixed. And you might need to accept that I'm one of those."

Chapter Eleven

Rory stilled beside her. "You think I'm trying to fix you? Is that why you left today?"

She gave him an imploring stare. "Well, aren't you?"

Rory ran a hand over his hair and shook his head. Had he been that obvious or that arrogant? "No. This isn't about *fixing* a person, Vanessa. Me, reaching out to you, at first, it was all about the pain I saw in your eyes. I *did* want to fix that maybe. That's my calling. That's my job. My hope. I want you to feel God's love and know that you're not alone. I want you to be happy. But I understand that I can't *fix* you. Being a minister, a man of God, doesn't mean I have all the answers. There are no easy answers. But I can help people who are in pain. Because I know that kind of pain."

"Why?" she asked. "Why do you know that kind of pain? Why can't you open up to me the way you expect me to open up to you?"

Rory sat in stunned silence. No one had ever turned the tables on him before. Most people were so glad to have someone to talk to in confidence that they never suspected their minister might have suffered at some point in his life. And Rory certainly never offered up his life story.

"You see," she said, nodding when he didn't answer her question. "How can you expect me to pour out my soul to you when you can't be honest with me? I've had too many people in my life who withheld things from me, Rory. I don't even know my father. Never even saw the man. And I really didn't know my mother. But I learned from her…and from the lifestyle she chose. I can't live like that. I'm afraid to hope because I'd probably be a horrible wife and a terrible mother. And I don't think God can help me change."

"But He can," Rory said, shocked that she'd become so bitter and jaded. "I never knew either of my biological parents," he said, giving in, crossing a line. "And I fell in love once before. But that didn't last either. So I decided to serve my country, but I joined the army for all the wrong reasons. Until God showed me the one right reason for being there. I could help people who thought they were beyond help."

Tears misted in her eyes. "I'm sorry. My problems are small, really, compared to all of that."

"No, Vanessa." He grabbed her hand. "To God, no one's problem is small. He can handle it. He can take the smallest problem or the biggest problem onto His shoulders." Staring over at her, he added, "It's not the size of the problem. It's the strength of our faith that matters. No matter the problem and no matter the outcome. Good or bad, God will see us through."

"But how will I know if He's willing to do that for me?" she asked, tears moving down her cheeks.

He touched a hand to her arm and then pointed to his heart. "That has to come from inside you. You have to allow Him into your heart. And when it happens, you won't have to do anything. You'll know. You'll feel it and your life will change."

"How do I reach that point?" she asked. "How do I become more like you? Truly happy and truly thankful?"

"You're doing it right now, here in this house. Step by step, day by day. You have to open yourself up to the possibilities. You have to accept that in God's eyes, you matter."

She looked so surprised he wanted to take her in his arms and reassure her. "You'll get through this but it won't be easy. It might take a few days, or weeks or years, even. Grief is a never-ending process. You've lost your mother, but you've also lost a part of yourself. I think part of your grief stems from not knowing a lot of things, of what might have been, what could have been. You can't find peace or closure because you've never had those things in the past. You're left with a lot of questions."

Her eyes widened, as if a lightbulb had gone off. But then the light in her eyes dimmed again. "Will I ever have that feeling, Rory? That feeling of standing in a beautiful garden, in the sunshine, with love all around me?"

"I hope so," he said. Then he did reach for her. He took her into his arms and hugged her close. "I've never done this before. I'm trying so hard not to cross that line. I want you to trust me."

She pulled back and gave him a wobbly smile. "I do trust you, more than I've ever trusted anyone. But that scares me."

Rory's eyes met hers. "It doesn't have to be scary." He wanted to kiss her and tell her about how his feelings were changing each time he was around her. "I don't want to scare you. I want to make you feel better."

He couldn't stop the feelings coursing through him. He pulled her close and held her. "I'm afraid, too, Vanessa.

I'm afraid to share things with you. I'm afraid to give in to you. You'll leave and I'll be alone again."

She pulled back to stare up at him with misty eyes. "You were in love once?"

"Yes."

"And it ended badly?"

He closed his eyes to the scenes in his head. "Yes."

"You don't have to talk about it, Rory," she said. "I understand."

He pulled her back into his arms. "It was a long time ago."

They didn't speak for a while. He held her there and savored the quiet of having someone to hold. Even while the weight of his guilt tried to drag him back down.

Finally, she pulled away and wiped her eyes. "Thank you."

Rory touched a finger to her moist cheek. "You're going to pull through. You're safe now. We're all with you. We're all praying for you."

"I know," she said. "I can feel it." She touched a hand to her heart. "Here."

After telling her good-night, Rory stepped out into the moonlight and stared up at the heavens.

I'm in deep here, Lord. I could use some grace and guidance.

Because he didn't want to watch Vanessa walk away again.

She was in church the next day. And she waited to talk to him after the sermon. "I've decided I can't rush this. So I'm staying here a little longer than I'd planned." She pushed at her hair and looked out at the lake. "I'll be here for a few weeks at least."

He wanted to do a fist pump, but he refrained. "That's probably a good idea. The rummage and estate sales are at the end of next week, and that'll be exhausting. Give yourself time to get through that and then rest up for a while. This is a good place to heal, I promise."

"I'm beginning to see that," she said. "I'm sorry about how I left the cookout, but I appreciate you checking on me last night." She shrugged. "I've already talked to Marla about it, and she made me feel better about things. She went through a lot of grief when her husband was killed and Gabby had such an ordeal." Glancing around, she said, "Thank you for checking on me."

"Of course," he said. He wanted to add, "Anytime." But he was beginning to think in terms of "All the time."

Two little kids ran by, squealing and giggling. Vanessa whirled to stare at them. "So full of energy. That's another thing that scares me about ever having children. I'm not equipped to handle all the needs of a child. Maybe I shouldn't volunteer to be a mentor since I'm not practiced in that area."

"They can be intimidating," Rory said. But he didn't buy that she'd never want children or that she wouldn't be good with children. Kandi might help in that area—if she didn't mow down Vanessa before they ever got to know each other. They'd made progress the first time they'd met, but being a mentor to a troubled teen took staying power. If Vanessa got close to Kandi and then left out of fear, they'd both suffer for it. So he hoped she'd dive right in with the youth program. She'd have to explain to Kandi that it would only be for a few weeks, but they could be friends for life.

"I liked your sermon," Vanessa said, her eyes following the children as they chased each other around the church yard.

He'd talked about coming to God with the attitude of a little child—open and honest and inquisitive, full of possibility and hope. He wished for that kind of acceptance and grace in Vanessa's life.

"I'm glad you decided to come today," he said. "And that you liked the message."

She gave him a soft smile. "Well, I've got a busy afternoon. Tagging, bagging and dragging."

He laughed and almost offered to help her. But he was going to step back and let her decide how much she wanted from him. It was the only way. "Then I guess I'll see you Wednesday night. I have some shut-ins to visit today."

Rory waved to her once she was on the other side of the street and saw the light from the afternoon sun casting her in golden whitewashed rays. She looked beautiful, standing there.

She was staying a while longer. That gave him hope. Because he'd felt it again today, standing beside her on the church steps. The kind of love that felt so beautiful, it pierced through the hardest of hearts. The kind of love that faith brought to a relationship.

He'd almost forgotten how that could feel.

"I want that," he said into the sun. Then he closed his eyes and took a deep breath and allowed himself to hope again.

Because now, he was thinking he wanted that with her.

On Monday morning, Rory's office phone jingled. When he didn't hear Barbara picking up, he remembered she had a doctor's appointment this morning. So he grabbed for the phone on the third ring. "Hello?"

"Oh, hi. I was hoping to talk to Barbara."

Vanessa.

"Hi. She's out for an appointment. How are you?"

"I'm better," she said. "Got a lot done yesterday."

"That's good. We're bringing stuff out this week and next. We store donations in the back of Alec's big warehouse and move them over here for the sale in our gathering hall."

"I'm almost ready, too," she said. "But I'm calling about Kandi, and I thought Barbara might have an answer. Did I ever get cleared to be her mentor?"

Rory sat up straight. "I'm pretty sure you did. I'll call Wanda and find out for sure. Are you coming Wednesday night?"

"I thought I would. For a midweek break and because I've been where she is and I thought maybe I could at least listen to her and encourage her while I'm here."

"I think that's a great idea," he said, lifting his eyes heavenward in a thankful prayer. "At least she's not seeing that boy anymore, according to Wanda."

"I hope not. They could be sneaking around though."

"I know." He prayed not. "I'll call Wanda and get back to you, but I don't think it'll be a problem. Kandi needs positive adult role models."

"Not sure I'm that, but I'll try."

She sounded kind of down. He wished he could make her see her worth. "You're more than qualified."

"If you count the school of hard knocks."

"Been there, got the diploma," he retorted. "Believe me, that counts for a lot."

"One day you'll have to explain that to me but only when you're ready."

He laughed, thinking she might be dropping him a hint to give her time, too. "It's a long story." Then he hesitated and took a deep breath. "Are we okay, you and me?"

A pause. "Yes, why wouldn't we be?"

He let out a sigh. "I don't know. I mean, I hugged you the other night."

"Don't you hug a lot of your church members?"

"Yes, but they don't all feel as good in my arms as you do."

Her smile held a hint of mischief and a dollop of doubt. "Are we doing something forbidden, Rory?"

"Not that I know of. I might be a preacher, but I'm still a man and… I'm attracted to you."

When she didn't respond, he thought he'd lost her again. But finally she said, "It felt good, being in your arms."

"So are you staying here a while longer because…in part because of that?"

"Maybe. That and Kandi and the house and a thousand different reasons."

"Well, I'm glad I might be one of them."

"I'll talk to you later."

He sure hoped so. "I'll see you later this week."

Vanessa checked the bag she'd bought this afternoon. She'd been approved to mentor Kandi, so she'd bought the teen all kinds of girlie stuff. Lotions and nail polish, earrings and a colorful necklace and a tie-dyed scarf. She'd even thrown in some books, young-adult type stories that the salesclerk had assured her would be suitable for a girl Kandi's age.

Time to go. Her nerves rattled a protest, which was silly. Just talk with Kandi and visit with everyone. It would do her good to get out of her gloom to try and help someone. Or so she told herself.

And she'd see Rory there, of course.

But she also reminded herself that she'd made a solemn vow never to have children. She didn't want to put a child through some of the things she'd endured. She was so afraid she'd turn out like her mother. Vanessa didn't think she had what it would take to raise a child.

She knew she needed to focus on something besides her own problems. And the preacher. She had to stop thinking about Rory. Something had happened between them the other night. Something that was soft and soothing but also exciting and intriguing. She'd never felt that way in a man's arms before.

Cherished.

Rory made her feel cherished. He was willing to fight for her, and Vanessa had never known that feeling before either.

But she couldn't stay here, waiting for what might or might not develop between them.

And yet there he was, front and center, when she entered the gathering hall. He looked so unpreacher-like in his faded khaki shorts and chambray button-up shirt. Now *he'd* make a great father. He loved this group.

Vanessa sent up a prayer for strength. She seemed to have a big crush on the preacher. But ministers did have a personal life, so she shouldn't feel so guilty.

Mainly, she needed him to tell her what had happened with his first love. And she had to explain to him that she might not be the marrying, settling-down kind. No matter how she felt in his arms.

She looked around and saw Kandi talking to some other teens. So she headed that way, giving Rory a wave as she went.

"Hi," she said when she neared Kandi.

The girl wore old overalls over a black T-shirt, her high-top sneakers scuffed and worn but ultra cool in pink-and-black checks. She had on huge pink Lucite earrings.

"Hey." Kandi tried to look nonchalant but gave up. "What's in the bag?"

Vanessa smiled. "It's for you. Rory—I mean Preacher—told me I've been cleared to be your official mentor. So I celebrated." She offered the bag to Kandi.

But the girl looked embarrassed. "I didn't ask for a mentor."

Vanessa could tell she'd moved in too quickly. "I know. I mean, I volunteered. I want to get to know you. I'll be leaving soon anyway, so you'll only have to put up with me for a few more weeks."

"Yeah, whatever." Kandi took the bag. "Thanks." Then she shrugged and walked off with the other girl who'd been fascinated by this whole exchange.

Vanessa turned, thinking she'd leave in humiliation.

"Don't go out that door."

Rory. Had he seen that whole exchange?

Chapter Twelve

"She's not interested. Did I do something wrong?"

"No, you did everything right. And she's interested. She's not used to people being kind to her."

"That's a horrible way to live."

He guided her toward the buffet line. "And yet, a lot of children learn to live that way. It's called survival mode."

"I guess I have a little of that in me," she admitted, thinking he'd probably learned his own survival test, too. And obviously neither of them wanted to delve too deeply into the past. "I hurt for her, Rory. How can I reach her?"

Rory watched the corner of the long room where the pack of teens had gathered. "By being here. Wanda told her you were her new mentor, but she's playing hard to get. That's what she does, and most people give up or ask for another kid to work with." He eyed Kandi. "It's hard to trust when you've been let down so much."

Again, Vanessa got the impression he'd been there himself. "I guess I have to *earn* her trust, right?"

"Yes, so don't take it personally. We all go through that, don't we?"

"Touché," Vanessa said. "But you're right. And I was thinking pretty much the same thing about myself. You and I—we're still in that stage, that learning-to-trust stage." She shrugged. "I was kind of snarky when I first met you."

He did an eyebrow quirk, his eyes full of mirth. "Really? I don't recall."

"Right." She couldn't stop the low laugh. "I was a real pill."

"Well, you're better now," he said. He gave her one of those blue-eyed hopeful glances. "And we're both getting there. Let's eat and laugh and have fun. She'll come around when she sees her tactics aren't working on you."

Vanessa wondered about that. Kandi had enough attitude to launch a ship. But Vanessa remembered her own hard times and how she'd acted out and rebelled. Bigtime. She also wondered if she and Rory would ever be able to trust each other enough to truly open up about everything that had brought them to this point.

She had him figured out a little more now. He counseled and consoled others, but he didn't believe he was worthy of asking someone to listen to him. He was a good man. A kind and loving man, but she couldn't help but see that he didn't seem to expect those traits in return from others. Rory shielded his own hurts and pains behind that cheery, positive facade. He put others ahead of his own needs, an admirable trait. But it was also a front that protected him from the world. He needed to heed some of his own advice.

Because wasn't that a horrible way to live, too? Keeping your own hurts buried away while you counseled everyone else? Especially for a man of God?

Vanessa knew there was always a reason for such behavior. Her past was one of the main reasons she didn't want to risk settling down and having children of her own. What was Rory's reason for deflecting love from himself?

She thought about Kandi and decided for now she'd have to concentrate on that. "It takes one to know one," she said to Rory in a quiet whisper.

"Maybe," he replied. "And it might take one to win one over, too." He gave her a soft smile. "One who understands and can be a positive role model in her life. One who has survived and thrived in spite of everything."

"You give me too much credit," she said. "I'm trying to get on with my life."

"I give you a *lot* of credit," he replied. "I admire you, and I'm proud that you're willing to put aside your discomfort and personal feelings to help a troubled young girl."

She was proud of him, too. But Vanessa also hurt for him. She suddenly wanted to know the real Rory Sanderson, flaws and all. "You got me into this," she said on a low, soft note. "I don't want to let you down."

His gaze washed over her with a tender longing. "That won't happen."

Vanessa followed him and filled her plate with spaghetti and French bread. "Maybe I just came for the food. This smells wonderful."

"Wanda's homemade spaghetti," he said, piling his plate full. "She cooks it for days. And if it got you here…"

Vanessa laughed at his lifted eyebrows. "Amazing."

He grinned like a school kid. "Marla sometimes provides food, too."

"I'll gain ten pounds, being here."

He laughed at that, but his gaze slid over her in a warm flow. "You'll be fine." Whirling, he called out. "Round up, people, so we can bless the food and then eat the food."

Relieved that they'd moved on to another subject, Vanessa found a round table where an older man sat with a teenaged boy. Rory grabbed a seat next to her. "Vanessa, this is Paul Middleton and Johnny Thomason."

"Hi." Vanessa managed a smile, her instincts still telling her to bolt.

The man spoke to her, but the boy nodded and went back to eating, a sullen expression on his face. So maybe she wasn't the only one experiencing difficulties with this.

"Mentor and mentee?" she whispered to Rory.

"Yep. And yours should be here any minute."

Vanessa glanced around. "What if she left?"

"She can't leave without her foster parents."

Vanessa tried to eat, but the bread stuck in her throat. Why did she have to go and get involved? She couldn't help anyone. She was too confused and messed up to know what kind of advice to give to a teen.

She'd have to tell Rory she'd changed her mind. And she'd have to learn to avoid him and those beseeching blue eyes, too.

But a swish of air and a plop next to her caused her to look around. Kandi made a lot of noise getting into her seat, but she had the bag of goodies in one hand and her plate of food in the other. Her frown dared anyone to question her.

Vanessa glanced at Rory. He gave her a quick smile and then turned to the young girl. "Hey, Kandi. What you got there?"

"As if you didn't know," Kandi retorted. Then she stared over at Johnny. "Did you get a bagful of fingernail polish?"

Johnny looked unsure about how to respond. He had

fine blond hair with long bangs that hid his eyes. He shrugged. "I dunno."

"I brought Johnny some books," Mr. Middleton said. "I heard he likes to read."

Johnny looked mortified. He kept his eyes on his plate.

Kandi laughed. "I got some books, too. Can't wait to read them."

The sarcasm fairly dripped from her words.

Mr. Middleton tried again. "Books can change your world. The more you read, the more you can learn and grow. A good book can help solve a lot of the world's problems."

Johnny looked relieved but Kandi gave a little snort. Then she turned to Vanessa. "Hey, thanks for the bag. It's almost like Christmas around here."

Vanessa glanced at Rory. He nodded in encouragement, so she dived right in. "I'm glad my gift makes you feel like it's Christmas," she said to Kandi. "But I'm not here just to give you gifts. I'm here because I know how it feels to be all alone and scared and confused—"

"I'm not confused and I'm not scared," Kandi said. Then she got up and walked away, leaving her food and the bag behind.

"I'll walk you home."

"You don't have to do that," Vanessa said, wishing the last couple of hours could have gone a little better. "I'm going to help clean the kitchen and… I can find my way home."

"I'll meet you at the door when you're finished," he said, his tone determined.

Vanessa nodded, deciding she wouldn't argue with him right now. She hurried to the kitchen and soon had her hands immersed in soapy dishwater. The dishwasher was already full and running, so she was washing these few big pieces by hand.

Kandi walked up and picked up a dish cloth. "I'll dry," she said, her scowl belying the polite offer.

Vanessa didn't hide her surprise. "Now you decide to talk to me?"

"I'm drying dishes, not talking," Kandi said, still stubborn, still full of bite.

"Oh, okay." Vanessa scrubbed a baking sheet with renewed determination.

"I think it's clean," Kandi said with a smirk.

"I don't know." Vanessa wanted to show a bit of her own attitude. "I still see a few grease spots."

"Those have been there forever," Kandi retorted. "They won't come out, no matter how hard you scrub them." Then she whirled to stare at Vanessa. "I'm sorry I was rude to you. I like the stuff you gave me."

Vanessa tried not to show too much enthusiasm, but the comment about those dark spots on the baking sheet stayed with her. "Okay."

"Wanda told me I needed to say that."

"Of course."

The girl did a fabulous eye roll. "But… I'm sorry. Really. You put some pretty cool stuff in that bag." She wiped the baking sheet dry. "I might even read that book. Looks like it could be good."

"I'm glad to hear that," Vanessa said. "Wanda invited me to come by her house sometime. So you and I can have some quality time together."

"Yeah. Whatever." Kandi threw down the dish towel. "Later."

"Later," Vanessa called. Then she grinned. Big.

And looked up to find Rory grinning back at her.

* * *

Rory wanted Vanessa to trust him. *Him.* Not just the preacher in him, but the man he'd become. So when they reached her porch, he pointed to the big glider hidden behind some overgrown jasmine bushes. "Let's sit a minute, okay?"

She looked unsure. "What is it?"

"Nothing." He took her by her hand. "I think we need to talk."

"I did something wrong, didn't I?" She fell onto the old metal glider, causing it to squeak and groan in protest. "Did Kandi's foster mom tell you to never bring me back to the youth meetings?"

He smiled and shook his head. "No. In fact, she wants you to come to visit with Kandi next week. Maybe Tuesday night?"

Vanessa looked shocked and pleased, all at the same time. "I'll see if I can clear my schedule." When he squeezed in beside her, she asked, "Is that what you wanted to talk to me about?"

"No." He took in a deep breath, the scent of her floral perfume warring with the smell of jasmine and gardenia. "I wanted to tell you…about me."

She looked surprised again. "Really? I mean, everything?"

"Maybe," he said, dread in the one word. "I need you to understand how I feel, how I can identify with you and Kandi and all of the other foster kids we try to help."

Vanessa took his hand, her fingers curling against his with a grip that felt sure and strong. "I want to hear all about you."

Rory nodded and stared out into the moonlight. He could hear the distant sound of the lake's gentle waves hitting the shore in a never-ending tug. "I told you I was a foster child. I never knew my real parents, and I wasn't adopted until I was older. I always thought something was wrong with me since no one wanted me. But when my parents brought me home, my mom told me that there was nothing wrong with me. She said God had been waiting to find the perfect family for me. And she told me how long she and my dad had waited to have a child."

"She sounds like a wonderful person," Vanessa said. "Did you…do you love them?"

"Yes." He could admit that easily. "They were older than most who adopt, but they gave me a good life. My father was retired military, gruff and demanding but fair and always willing to listen. When he died, I fell back into this kind of despair. But we got through it, Mom and me."

He wasn't sure he could do this. So he stopped and took another long breath.

"It's hard," Vanessa said. "Death is hard because it doesn't give you a second chance."

"Right." Rory certainly understood that concept, but he knew death was another phase. "It's final here on earth. But God promises us we will all be reunited in Heaven." He touched her hand. "That's our second chance. Seeing our loved ones again in eternity."

Vanessa looked down. "Do you think my mom is in Heaven, Rory?"

Rory heard this question a lot. "I didn't know your mother, but I'm hoping you will see her in Heaven, yes."

"But you can't promise me that?"

"I can't, no. But Christ promises those who follow Him eternal life."

Vanessa gulped a deep breath. "I wish I could have talked to her before she died. By the time I got there, she was already in a coma. I was so angry and bitter and awful."

Rory stopped talking and pulled her into his arms. She felt fragile and delicate, but he'd seen the steel she'd placed around her heart. "I don't have all the answers, but we can always hold out hope that everyone we love had a change of heart toward the end of life and will be there waiting for us. I hope your mother felt your presence there in her last hours."

Vanessa lifted her head and looked into his eyes. Rory forgot the rest of his story. He wiped at her tears and then he leaned down and kissed her. Vanessa's lips were soft and silky. She pulled her hand through his hair and tugged him closer.

Rory became lost in the kiss, lost in her touch, lost in what this felt like, holding a woman in his arms.

And he knew without any doubt that Vanessa could be the one for him. But how in the world could he ever convince her of that?

But it wasn't about convincing Vanessa. He had to let go of all the things he'd been holding to so tightly, too. So he pulled back and touched a hand to her face. "I can't do this, Vanessa. Not yet. I'm not ready to let go of my secrets, because it'll be like saying goodbye to the woman I loved all over again."

He hated the hurt and fear in her eyes. "Rory…?"

"I'm sorry." He kissed her again, and then he got up and went back to his side of the street.

Chapter Thirteen

Friday morning. Vanessa yawned and glanced around the house. She still had a long way to go, but things were shaping up. She had another week until the church rummage sale and her estate sale. Then she'd be forced to fling the doors of this home open to the public.

And watch part of her life go out the door. But maybe that was for the best. Rory had kissed her Wednesday, and then he'd told her he was sorry, just up and walked away. She hadn't slept much in the last couple of nights.

So what did she do now? He'd made her care and now he couldn't deal? Or had he stopped things before they went any further because he didn't want to hurt her? Or watch her leave?

They'd hit a snag. And she thought she knew what that snag was all about. He was reliving his past, too. A past that involved loving and losing another woman. Vanessa figured that if she hadn't come along, he'd have stayed trapped behind that brilliant facade for the rest of his life.

"My turn to minister to you, Preacher."

But right now, she had to finish up things here. The busywork would help her sort through her feelings for Rory much in the same way she'd sorted through her own secrets for the last few weeks. In the meantime, she hoped he'd come back around.

"So not fair. So wrong." Vanessa shook her head, determined to stop mumbling and get on with things.

He'd been patient with her. She would do the same for him.

Staring at the big, cluttered kitchen, she wished she'd cleared out this room already. But when she'd started, she'd crashed and burned out on the sidewalk with Rory watching her. That day, she didn't know him well enough to tell him her fears and concerns or why she'd become so upset. She wasn't sure she could tell him anything more now either. But this kitchen represented so much of the struggle between Vanessa and her mother. The silent meals. The shouting matches. The clashing of dishes. The burned food. The lost hope. This would be another hurdle. One more thing to clean up and tuck away.

And then she'd have to tackle the last bedroom. Her old bedroom. She had a lot to overcome before she put this house on the market. Up until now, Vanessa had believed all of her nightmares were holding her back. But it was more than that now.

Vanessa thought about Rory and how he'd tried to open up to her the other night. And he'd kissed her. That first kiss had left a lasting impression on Vanessa, like an imprint that marked her as cherished and special. They'd kissed several times, there in the rickety old glider, until he'd bolted like a forest animal on the run. Rory brought her the kind of security and comfort she'd only hoped for in her dreams. Now, he needed to feel that same kind of security. Or did he already?

"What are *you* afraid of, Rory?"

How could she ever forget Rory and his kisses? Could

she make him see that he needed her as much as she needed him?

Because daydreams had replaced a lot of her nightmares. Daydreams of being with Rory, which seemed impossible. So here she stood, wondering what to do next.

Maybe she should ask Rory how to handle all of these mixed-up, scary feelings. Marla had urged her to do that from the beginning. As a minister, he was bound to keep what she told him between them, and he'd listened to a lot of her rants already.

But as a friend, as a man she was attracted to, he should be the last person she needed to confide in. He had opened up to Vanessa about his past until the kissing had taken over and stopped the soul sharing. Then he'd practically run away screaming. But she needed to hear everything about him, good and bad. She needed to be honest with him, too.

Rory had become too important to her, even after she'd fought against her growing feelings for him.

Giving up, she called Marla. "Rory kissed me."

A soft squeal and then a giggle. "This is interesting."

"Yes, but he took himself back across the street after he kissed me. Couldn't get away fast enough."

"Did you two fight?"

"No. We kissed. A lot." Vanessa sipped on her bottle of water while she stood at the big window and stared over at the church. "I…I finally gave in to all these feelings and now…he's hiding out over there in his sanctuary."

She heard a cash register dinging. Marla was at work. Vanessa wished she had a cupcake.

"Have you talked to him since the kissing session?"

"No." Vanessa turned away from the window. "No. I'm giving him time to think about things." Then she took a deep breath. "So you don't know what happened? In his past?"

Marla didn't speak for a minute. Then Vanessa heard, "Thank you, Mr. Houston. Give Miss Becky a hug for me." A customer. Marla's Marvelous Desserts stayed busy.

"I should let you get back to work," Vanessa said, the image of white icing covering rich chocolate enticing her.

"No. I'm on my way back to the office," Marla replied. "Now, I can talk without my gossip-loving staff listening in."

Vanessa took in some air and then rushed on. "So you do know something?"

"No. I only know that he served at a small church near Crestview before he enlisted in the army and went through training to become a chaplain."

"Did he serve over there with any of his current buddies?"

"No," Marla said. "They all met here, remember. He was army and Alec and Blain were marines—even though I called Alec Soldier Boy when we first met, but now that's our special joke with each other. And Hunter, well, no one talks much about what Hunter did. Some kind of black ops, maybe."

Vanessa realized she had a lot to learn about Rory's friends. But she needed to learn more about him first. "He said he'd loved someone and it ended badly."

"Preacher?" Marla seemed as surprised as Vanessa had been. "He's never mentioned that around me. Are you sure?"

"I know—hard to believe. Yes, that's what he said. I think he's buried his feelings so deep, no one can find them. Not even him." Vanessa turned back to the window. "And now that I'm here and he kissed me...well, something is sure bubbling to the surface. But he's having a hard time. He pushed me to open up, and I'm getting better at talking about my life and now he's the one who's clamming up. Or shutting down. Or whatever you want to call it."

"I'm glad you're here," Marla said. "You sound stronger every day and, well, we've all been praying for Rory to find a soul mate, someone to love him. He has so much love to give. It sounds as if you and he have something, Vanessa. Don't give up on him. Don't give up on yourself either."

"I believe he cares," Vanessa said. "And I'm beginning to care about him. More than I want to care. I don't know if I'm worthy of his love."

"You are," Marla said. "Rory needs you, and God wants you to feel worthy, too. You and Rory could be so wonderful together."

After they talked a few more minutes, Vanessa hung up, more confused than ever. But maybe Marla was right. If God had a plan for their lives, she prayed He'd reveal it soon. Because it would be so hard to fall for Rory and then have to leave him.

"What's up with you?"

Rory turned from the porch railing and the view of the full moon hanging over the bay to find Hunter Lawson propped up against a door frame at the AWOL camp house, his face in the shadows.

"I'm admiring the moon," Rory replied to Hunter's question. "What's up with you?" And did he really want to hear the answer to that question?

"I'm wondering why the man who planned this grand bachelor party is staring up at the moon. We've got pizza and wings, cold drinks and old movies. And you promised games."

Hunter rarely said more than one-word comments and now this. The third degree?

"It's all there," Rory said, turning to shove past Hunter's stoic stare. "Hey, Blain, want us to help you make a wedding dress out of toilet paper?"

Blain Kent stayed on the couch but lifted one dark eyebrow. "I think I'll have to pass on that one, brother."

Rory grinned. "Barbara said that's what they do at girlie bridal showers. Just asking. We could make you a duct-tape tuxedo."

Alec got up to get another slice of pizza. "What are we supposed to do at bachelor parties, anyway?"

"Not what they do in Vegas," Rory said, nodding toward the movie they'd been watching. "This is a regular get-together before Blain here goes off the market. Same as we do every week but with more feeling."

Hunter grunted. "Two down and one to go." He pointed his can of soda toward Rory. "'Cause I'm thinking you've got it bad, man."

"You left yourself off that list," Rory retorted.

"I don't have any aspirations on that account," the Okie replied in a steady, sure voice.

Blain and Alec glanced at each other and then back to Rory.

"Do *you* have aspirations, Preacher?" Blain asked, his dark eyes now full of interest.

"I aspire to turn up the music on this party," Rory said. He'd been looking forward to this for a while now, and they'd planned it a week before the wedding since Blain had a lot going on next week. But his heart wasn't in it. And he could tell that his buddies could tell. He wanted this to be a festive, joyous night, since the wedding would be the Sunday after the rummage sale.

Next weekend. Vanessa might leave after that.

Or she'd probably go sooner, after the way he'd left things the other night. The way he'd left her.

"Let's go for a boat ride," Alec said, getting up to throw away his paper plate. "Full moon. Nice wind. Good for the soul."

Rory watched Alec. The limp he'd sustained due to being injured while he'd been deployed a couple of years ago was just about gone. Even the scar on Alec's face was less noticeable now. But Rory knew some scars never went away.

"Okay, a boat ride." He nodded. "That was next on the agenda anyway."

Blain got up and finished his drink and then poked Rory in the chest. "And while we're out there, maybe we'll hold you under until you tell us what's on your mind."

An hour later, they sat rocking in Alec's sleek boat, the moon laughing down on them while a balmy breeze moved over the blue-black, soothing waves. So far, so good. They hadn't dunked him yet.

Hunter sat off to the side with his legs propped up, looking back at the shore.

Blain and Rory sat opposite each other on the wrap-around seats while Alec stayed at the helm.

"Are we having fun now?" Rory asked.

"Yep." Hunter didn't even turn around.

"More fun than a kangaroo on a trampoline," Blain replied.

Rory decided this was a good place to lay it on the line. "I kissed Vanessa the other night."

"An aspiration if ever I heard one," Alec said through

a grin. He twisted around on his seat. "So why aren't we celebrating?"

Rory rubbed a hand down his face. "I enjoyed kissing her. Too much."

"Is there such a thing as too much kissing?" Blain asked. "I sure hope not."

Alec sat still. "Go on, Preacher."

"I think I'm falling for her, but we have a lot to work through."

Blain and Alec both lifted their drinks in a mock toast.

"Been there, got married," Alec said.

"Been there, about to get married," Blain added.

"Never been there. Ain't gonna happen," Hunter said into the wind.

Rory loved their dry wit. "I was married once."

The boat stopped rocking.

Hunter turned around.

The moon became a spotlight.

Alec twisted away from the wheel and came back to the stern. "Say that again."

Rory couldn't take back the confession, so he went on. "I was young. Just out of seminary. About to start my career at a small-town church. We were happy. And then I was alone and I struggled and then because I was so angry, I joined the army and thought I'd take out my frustrations. And we all know how that went. I found my calling again, but I'm still alone. And I feel guilty for kissing one woman when I can't let go of another one."

"What happened?" Blain asked. "I mean, to the first woman."

Even now, Rory couldn't say the words. "Life happened."

He left it at that, and his friends left him to his silence.

Finally, Hunter grunted. "It's always something, man."

But he touched Rory on the arm before he turned his face back to the sea.

Alec moved back to the cockpit and cranked the boat, and they listened to her purr for a few seconds. "I suggest you take advantage of those kisses, my friend," he said over his shoulder to Rory. "Don't run away from a second chance. Turn back toward her and fight. You're a fighter, Preacher. But you have a different weapon than most. You are more of a warrior than anyone I know."

They went silent again for a few minutes.

Blain nodded and let out a hoot. "Well, since I'm the one about to turn toward the woman that *I* love, how about we take this baby for a spin and see what she's got?"

Rory finally grinned, and strangely, he felt better. "Let's go."

Hunter grunted again. "Glad we had this chat."

And they were off into the night, laughing and talking about all the things they rarely talked about. Including women.

When they slowed at the marina, Alec cut the engine again.

And Rory finally told them the story of his young wife and her death.

Chapter Fourteen

He was giving her the space she needed, and now she missed having him around. Saturday and Sunday had come and gone. A long, silent weekend that Vanessa had tried to fill with work and cleaning up. She'd planned to attend church Sunday, hoping she'd hear some words of wisdom from the man she'd come to admire as a minister and as a friend. She felt so alone here in this big, rambling house. Instead, she'd gone for an early-morning walk around the lake, and then she'd come home and talked to her lawyer on the phone and processed more shipping instructions for some of the items she would be keeping.

Exhausted, she'd curled up on the big sofa early in the evening, hoping to get some sleep. But that hadn't worked. So she'd stayed up late last night working on the photos for her website. Now she was exhausted and cranky. Monday morning had never looked or felt so bad.

She glanced at her mother's journal lying on the big plank dining table. What if what she needed to hear was inside that journal? Why couldn't she open it?

Because the truth might be in there and Vanessa wasn't sure she was ready for the complete truth. It seemed too intimate and invasive to read her mother's journal and hear Cora's innermost thoughts. Her mother's accusations could be there, inked beside what they had for dinner and what she was wearing on her latest date. Vanessa couldn't bear to view the horror of her time in this house with Gregory Pardue, all spelled out in black and white. And yet, she needed to sit down and read the whole thing.

Didn't the Bible have a verse about the truth setting you free? Vanessa suddenly wanted to be free. She needed to be free if she wanted a chance with Rory, didn't she?

Touching a hand to the thick, worn journal, she shook her head. "Not yet."

She'd open it tomorrow after she got back from Kandi's house. Wanda had called her and set a time for her visit with Kandi. "And dinner," Wanda had added. "We'd love to have you stay and eat with us."

The last thing Vanessa wanted right now was to sit down with a big, rowdy family and eat a meal. But saying no would be impolite. The Peppermons were a wonderful couple who truly sacrificed for the sake of helping children in need.

She reminded herself that if she'd had someone like that in her life growing up, she might be a different person today.

You do have someone like that now.

You have Marla and Alec and Aunt Hattie and Marla's parents. You have the Peppermons and Miss Fanny and you have Rory.

But she wouldn't have Rory or any of the other people who'd befriended her once she left here. She'd go back to New Orleans, and she'd be okay. She had friends there, and she had her work to keep her occupied.

But now that she'd experienced Millbrook Lake with different people, in a different time, she knew being okay—just okay—wouldn't ever be good enough again. Nor would working day and night. Nice, but not amazing.

That about summed it up. This place had turned into something amazing. She could almost be happy here. But she couldn't stay here, of course.

She'd miss the lake and kayaking, the ducks quacking and the seagulls cawing. She'd miss watching sailboats glide by or hearing speed boats charging along or children laughing in the park and dogs barking in return. Miss Fanny calling to her across the way, always with a smile and a kind word of encouragement and the beautiful music when the church choir was practicing. She'd miss the sweet smell of flowers and the earthy smell of the lake.

She'd miss that little white church across the street and the man who took care of everyone but himself.

I could be the one.

I could be the person who takes care of Rory.

No. Bad idea. Vanessa started digging through cabinets and dragging out old cookware and aged baking dishes. She'd never been one for settling down, married with children.

She wasn't maternal enough. She didn't want to turn out like her mother. She didn't want to bring a child into the world because she knew firsthand that little children weren't always protected in this world.

You'd never be like that. You'd be a good mother.

She could tell herself that all day long, but Vanessa would never believe it.

Gregory Pardue had told her something she'd never forgotten. "You're just like your mother. A big tease. A big dreamer. You aren't fit to be anyone's girlfriend or wife. You should plan on being alone all your life because no decent man will want you and you certainly won't be able to take care of any children."

He'd spouted all of those ugly things to her after he'd tried to molest her, in her room, here at this house.

A man of God, trying to molest his wife's only daughter.

Vanessa sat in the middle of the kitchen floor and stared at a scratch mark on the old cabinet door. And like all the pots and pans and old dish towels spilling out of the cabinets, her memories came tumbling out, cluttered and chaotic, cloying and stifling, much in the same way this house was beginning to stifle her with its secrets.

But she looked up and saw a brilliant ray of sunshine hitting on an old wall plaque that she'd never noticed before.

And her heart stopped and started beating in a fast-moving lift that echoed with each pulse inside her head.

"He heals the brokenhearted and bandages their wounds."

Psalm 147, Verse 3.

The tiny little square plaque had been varnished to a bright luster, but the black words were written in calligraphy on a stark white piece of canvas. Vanessa had no doubt that her mother had made this little sign and hung it there.

Her mother, who had never darkened the doors of a church. Even when she'd been married to a man who claimed to be a minister.

Vanessa got up and grabbed the plaque off the wall and held it close. Then she turned it over and saw the initials on the back.

CDT. Cora Donovan Tucker. Cora had created this after she'd married Richard Tucker.

Her mother had died alone and brokenhearted in a

nursing home. But she'd been brokenhearted long before she became ill.

"Everyone left you," Vanessa said. "We all abandoned you."

Vanessa sat down and cried, the little plaque held tightly to her heart. Then she put the plaque back in its place and turned to find her mother's journal.

"I think it's time to clear away the real clutter, Mama."

The clutter that had to have been documented in this journal. Vanessa knew she needed to read this journal, good and bad, in order to heal her own broken heart.

She called Rory. "Will you come over? I…I need your help."

He immediately agreed. "Of course. Give me five minutes."

Rory was a decent man. He would help her deal with this. She needed to remember that. It could never work between them, no matter how much her heart ached with each day that passed. But he could help her right now, in this moment, when she needed him the most. And when it was time for her to go, she could go with his kindness and his kisses embedded in her memories.

Good memories replacing bad ones. She'd have that at least.

"I'm out for the day," Rory told Barbara as he hurried out of his office.

"Did someone die?"

He turned and shook his head. "No, but I think someone is having a crisis of faith. I have to go."

"I hope everything works out for her," Barbara said, guessing who that someone had to be. "Sending prayers to cover both of you."

"Thanks." He could use those prayers. He'd certainly been doing some serious soul searching himself. But right now, he hurried across the street to Vanessa's house and knocked on the door. After his full disclosure on the boat the other night, his friends had encouraged him to tell Vanessa everything.

Now Rory prayed for the courage to do that.

She opened the door in a slow, cautious way, one hand hiding her face from the late morning sun. Rory took one look at her and pulled her into his arms. "What's wrong?"

She burst into sobs and pulled back, trying to wipe at her tears in a frantic way. "Everything. I… I…need to get out of this house."

"I know just the place," he said. "Do you trust me?"

She bobbed her head and took on a gritty, determined expression.

"I'll get my truck."

She nodded again. "I'll meet you out front."

Rory ran back across the street to the garage apartment and quickly cranked his old truck. Soon he was parked in the driveway of Vanessa's house. When Miss Fanny came out on her porch and waved to him, he waved back but didn't go over to talk to her.

Instead, he ran up the steps to Vanessa's house. She opened the door before he could knock again. "Are you ready?"

"Yes." She had a big tote bag with her, and she held something else in her hand, too.

Her mother's journal.

"Where are we going?" Vanessa asked Rory a few minutes later. She'd stopped crying, but her eyes were red rimmed and swollen.

"A special place," he explained. "It's private and se-cluded. No one will bother us there."

She nodded and watched the signs. "I haven't gone anywhere outside of the city limits since I got here. Sorry

I fell apart, but I...I needed to get out of that house for a while."

He took one of her hands in his. "Understandable since you've been sorting and cleaning for three weeks now. And you haven't cried a lot in all of that time."

"Has it been three weeks?" Her surprise turned to resolve. "I have to get this done."

"Are you in such a hurry to leave?" he asked, wishing she wouldn't go at all. Wishing he hadn't left her sitting there the other night.

"Not so much now." She gave him a watery stare. "I need a couple of hours away from that place, and then I'll get back and finish up. I only have the kitchen and a couple of other rooms left."

But she'd need more than a couple of hours, Rory thought. He'd stall her all afternoon. She also needed rest, and she needed to let go and mourn.

When he pulled the truck up to the rustic square beach house that sat high up on pilings near the waters of the big bay, Vanessa glanced around and then back to him.

"What place is this, Rory?"

"We call it AWOL," he said. "This is the camp house I own with Alec, Blain and Hunter."

"I thought no women were allowed here. That's what Marla told me once."

"Darlin', we seem to be breaking that rule a lot lately. It's okay. We're only allowed to bring very special women out here. Alec brought Marla here and Blain brought Rikki here."

He almost added that they'd gone on to become couples and...they were making lives together now. But Rory didn't think Vanessa was ready for that. He wasn't sure right now if he was ready for that either. But he did owe her the truth, at least.

He got out and came around to open her door. She turned to stare up at him. But her question was somber. "Do you think I'm special?"

"Oh, you have no idea," he said. Then he kissed her on the forehead. "I think you're amazing."

She didn't move. She sat there staring up at him, her eyes clear now. "I'm not all that amazing."

Rory hugged her close. "Let's get you inside so I can feed you and pamper you and...listen to you."

Vanessa reached up a hand to touch his face. "You really are a true minister, Rory."

He nodded. "Thanks, and I'm thinking that today I'll certainly be earning that title, right?"

She dropped her hand away. "Yes. You're exactly what I need today." Then she took his hand and followed him up the path to the house.

Chapter Fifteen

Vanessa steeled herself against breaking down again. She wasn't a crier. Never had been. She held her emotions in check because she'd seen too much drama growing up. Her mother's theatrics had left her cold and wanting. And unable to love anyone.

She'd been trying to fill that void in her heart since the day she'd left Millbrook Lake. Now she could see that all of her excuses—wanting a peaceful life, not wanting children, needing her space and turning away from God—had been just that. Excuses.

And yet, her excuses held steady. She wasn't ready to relinquish control yet. She didn't want to lose control anymore today either. So she wiped at her tears and lifted her spine into a straight line. She had to hold it together, somehow.

Once they were upstairs on the deep plank porch that faced the bay, she wiped her eyes and took in the view. "I can see why this place is so special to you and your friends."

Palm trees rustled in the breeze, a couple so close to the porch and so tall and gangly, she could reach out and touch their fronds. Hibiscus bushes and bougainvillea vines graced the yard, their colorful blossoms shining in the sun. The porch was long and deep, a good place to sit, no matter the weather.

Vanessa felt safe here, away from the lake and the town. Safe, hidden, covered. Had she become that kind of person? The kind who cowered behind closed doors and drawn-together curtains? The kind who ran away to a place like New Orleans, where everyone left you alone if that's what you wanted? Yes. She'd become a reclusive, shy, scared human being. She didn't have it all together at all. At some point, she'd given up on having grand adventures or finding someone special.

Special. A special place for special people. Rory had brought her here…and it felt right.

She stared out at the big bay waters and remembered how much she'd enjoyed kayaking around the lake with Rory. Rory was an adventure all wrapped up in a great package. And that was the main reason she kept resisting him.

"I take care of the yard," Rory said from behind her. "Blain is in charge of the security system. And Alec, well, he foots the renovations. Oh, and Hunter comes and goes, but he's good with mechanical things and he's a stickler for clean sheets and towels. So he's in charge of laundry. We all take care of maintenance. And we take turns cooking or ordering pizza."

"Sounds like you make a good team."

"We're tight," Rory said, coming to stand beside her. "We formed a bond that can't be broken. We help each other, guard each other and…we trust each other."

She pivoted to the big glass doors he'd flung open. The house looked clean and efficient but seriously lacking in anything remotely feminine. No floral throw pillows, no bright pretty dishes, no potted plants or whimsical pictures on the walls. Just a minimalist, manly interior with worn leather furniture, chunky wooden tables and bar stools for extra seating. And the biggest flat-screen television she'd ever seen.

"I've never had friends like that," she said, her tote bag and her mother's journal held close to her stomach. "We moved around so much when I was growing up, and by the time my mom settled here, I was in full-out rebellious mode and I only wanted to finish high school and get out on my own."

"Do you have friends now?" he asked. "For when you get back to New Orleans? So I won't worry about you."

A twinge of regret hit her in the stomach. What would her life be like now? Without Rory in it?

"I have employees in the boutique. They're taking care of things while I'm here. I have people hired to help me run the online site, too. I don't know what I'd do without my team."

"A team," he said, taking her by the hand and pulling her inside the house. "I didn't ask about a team. I asked if you had friends."

Wow. He had a way of zooming right in on things.

"No." She dropped her bag and the journal onto the butcher-block counter and pretended to study the row of cabinets underneath the big side window. "I don't make friends."

"We all need friends."

"Do we?" She whirled to stare over at him, needing to put that shield back up between them. Now that she was here, alone with him, she wished she'd never called him for help. She didn't need rescuing. She didn't need him. "I've been self-sufficient since I was eighteen, even before that, really. I do okay on my own."

He didn't make a move. He stood there, his eyes holding hers. "How's that working for you right now?"

He had her there. She lowered her head and then glanced up at him. "Not so well."

Rory took another step, getting closer. "Why did you call me, Vanessa?"

She glanced at the journal. She should tell him to take her home, that this had been a mistake. That kissing him had been a mistake. But she needed someone to talk to, and Rory had tried to be her friend. He wanted to listen. He was good at listening even if he didn't want to kiss her again.

"I need to…" Her voice trailed off. "This isn't easy for me. I need to talk to someone I can trust."

"You know you can trust me."

"As a minister."

"As your friend, too."

She nodded. "Okay. I need to read my mother's journal. I want to see what she wrote about me, and what she wrote about the men she paraded in front of me, and about the one man who tried to ruin me forever."

Rory moved a little closer. "This one man—he was a minister?"

She lowered her head again, ashamed, embarrassed and mortified. Keeping her gaze downcast, she nodded.

Rory pulled her chin up, his face inches from hers. "You do not need to hide in shame anymore, Vanessa. Not with me. Not with God."

Her skin flared hot as she sent him a burning stare. "Where was God the day that man walked into my bedroom and pushed me up against a wall and…put his hands all over me? Where was God that day, Rory?"

Rory's heart hurt with all the agony of arrows hitting him in the chest. How did he answer that question?

"He was there, Vanessa. God's love can overcome anything."

"But how could He have been there?" she asked, whirling around, her hands flailing out in front of her. "How?"

"What did this man do to you? How far did it go?"

She gave Rory a hard glare. "You don't want to answer my questions, do you?"

"I'm working on that, but right now I want to know what this man did to you."

"He tried to kiss me, but it didn't get very far. But him touching me went way too far for me," she said, putting a hand to her mouth. "He'd always flirted with me, but I ignored him. When he and my mom started dating, he'd hug me a lot and it felt so creepy. But after they got married, he kept insisting I come to church. He had this little start-up church west of town. A storefront kind of thing because his credentials were almost nonexistent. I refused at first, but Mom talked me into it, telling me I'd make new friends. *He* tried to become my new friend, always hovering, always making sick jokes. He'd talk to me in soothing tones, telling me he knew what was best for me. I hated being around him."

She stopped and took a shuddering breath. "That day, he was angry with me for not showing up for some sort of youth rally. That's why he came into my room. Mom thought he was disciplining me for not attending his important get-together. But he wanted to make a point, I think. He wanted to prove that I was a bad person."

She looked up at Rory, as if half expecting him to question her, too. "I pushed at him and scratched his face. I told him to stop, and then I ran out of the room."

Rory schooled his expression while his insides boiled with rage. "And what happened next?"

"I went to my mom," Vanessa said, dropping both of

her hands down to her side and turning to stare into the dark fireplace. "I told her what he'd tried to do and how he'd been flirting with me, but she didn't believe me. Then he came out of my room and called me all kinds of names. He told me I'd never amount to anything because I was a liar and that no man would want me because I was unfit." She shook her head. "He implied I'd come on to him, of course."

Rory closed his eyes, his own questions ricocheting inside his brain with a pounding of despair. *Dear God, help me. Help me to say the right thing. Help her to heal, Lord. Show her Your grace and love.*

"And your mother didn't ask him about what he'd done? She never questioned that he was the one lying?"

Vanessa whirled around. "No. Instead, she asked me what *I'd* done to provoke him."

"What did you tell her?"

"I tried to tell her the truth. That'd he come into my room and shut the door and that he'd tried to kiss me and…that I had to push him away." Rory heard her gulping in a breath. "I kept trying to explain, but she looked so disappointed, so horrified. And he stood there, smug and sure. It was awful. Awful." Vanessa took in a heaving breath. "And the worst—she turned on me. I had to live in that house with both of them, condemning me, challenging me at every turn, isolating me to the point that I forgot how to make friends."

She stopped, her hand going to her mouth again. "I was so ashamed."

Rory saw her face go white, saw the panic in her eyes. He pointed. "Bathroom—down the hall to the right."

She took off running, already retching. He heard the door slam, heard her being sick. He wanted to go to her, hold her and tell her it would be all right. But he knew she didn't need to hear that right now. He understood why she'd turned away from him at first, why her attitude had been stilted and distant toward him. No wonder Vanessa hadn't trusted *his* motives. He'd tried to invite her in and had suggested she come to the youth meetings. His actions had been strictly on a friendly basis, a way to reach out to someone he sensed was hurting.

But to Vanessa, his actions had mirrored those of a man who'd abused her and scarred her.

Dear Lord, what can I do now? How do I reach her?

Rory waited in the silence of the quiet house, the sound of the bay's gentle waves hitting the shore echoing inside his head like a soothing lullaby while he prayed the prayer that would guide him past his own understanding. After a few minutes, he heard the faucet water running and then the door opened and she came out, still pale, her eyes red rimmed and swollen.

"I'm sorry," she said, pushing at her hair.

Rory moved across the room and took her into his arms. "Don't ever apologize for this, Vanessa. You did nothing wrong." He stepped back, his hands gentle on her wrists. "I'm the one who should be apologizing. I didn't understand what you'd been through when I first met you. I can see how my overtures to invite you to church must have frightened you."

"No," she said, shaking her head. "No. You're not him. You're not like him."

"You're right on that," Rory replied. "I'm not like him, but if I had him right here in front of me today, I'd become reduced to brawling like a street fighter. I'm pretty sure I'd pulverize him."

"You're not that kind of man," she said. "You went to war to help others, to serve others. You fight with a different kind of strength, Rory. You fight for the broken people of this world."

He thought of Alec's words to him. He didn't admit that up until the other night on that boat, he hadn't completely trusted anyone either. Some minister he was, holding back his own confessions and angst while he tried to take care of everybody else. His friends were the best. Understanding and undemanding. Now they knew all he had to share. He'd bared his soul there in the dark on that boat. But he was glad they all knew about his past. He wondered why he'd held back for so long.

Today, he was taking their advice. He was turning toward the woman he thought he could love for a long, long time. He would be a warrior for this woman.

Rory swallowed back the emotions brimming over in his mind. "I'm fighting for you right now. And I know God's fighting for you, too. He brought you back here for a reason. It might have taken a lifetime, but His timing is never wrong."

She looked up at Rory, her eyes overflowing with doubt and hurt and anger. "I'm afraid, Rory. Afraid to move on and find happiness. Afraid of my feelings for you. Afraid to read my mother's journal." She stalled out, her eyelids fluttering. "But mostly, I'm afraid to give myself over to God."

Rory tugged her toward the couch. "Sit. I'm going to make you something to eat, and then I'm going to tell you about how much God loves you and wants you in His arms."

"I don't think—"

"And something to drink. Hot tea or cold?"

"Water with lemon."

"We have lemons," he said, smiling at her. He got up and found bottled water and sliced a lemon and put ice in two plastic cups, his hands steady again now. Then he poured the water into both, grabbed some crackers and cheese and a bag of grapes and brought it all back to the coffee table.

"I can't eat," she said.

"It's okay. You'll eat when you're ready."

Then he sat down beside her and pulled her into his arms. "Cry on my shoulder, Vanessa. Scream at me, rant at me, do whatever you need to do, but know this. I am not going to judge you or condemn you. I care about you. And so does God."

Then he kissed the top of her head. "And about God's timing—He brought *you* into my life at just the *right* time. You've helped me see that I have some long-held issues that have been holding me back, too." Snuggling her close, he added, "And I think it's time that we both settle up."

Chapter Sixteen

Vanessa's heart stopped and then skidded into a fast beat. "Are you willing to lay it all out there between us, Rory?"

"Yes," he said. "I'm willing to tell you things I've never told anyone. Not even the friends I'd trust with my life. But those friends know everything now. And they encouraged me to talk to you. To be honest with you."

"And why me?" She had to know that this was real and that he wouldn't panic again. And she needed to know what was holding him back. "Do you think you can trust me?"

"Yes," he said again, his usually animated eyes turning solemn and somber. "I've needed someone like you in my life for a long time now. But like you, I was afraid to let go or to give in to God's plan for my life."

Surprised at this candid conversation and touched that he felt this way about her, Vanessa smiled for the first time since she'd had her meltdown earlier. "How do you know if I'm in that plan? What if I mess things up for you the way my mother accused me of messing up things for her?"

"Didn't your mother, with all her flaws and problems,

finally find a man who could love her and change her
and make her see that she'd damaged you?"

Vanessa's mind reeled from the implications of that
statement. "Marrying Richard did make it better for me,
yes, but she never saw that her actions had damaged me,
Rory. She might have found happiness and a husband who
brought her the security she always craved, but she never
once told me she was sorry for what she did to me. For
what that man—the other husband—did to me. I can't
forget that, and I sure don't have to forgive it."

"Forgiveness is the hardest part of following Christ,"
Rory said. "It never comes easy but you need to understand something about forgiveness, Vanessa. It's more
about helping you to heal and grow through grace than
it is about soothing the other person's feelings. Don't get
me wrong. When you forgive someone it releases them
from any guilt or debt. But it also releases you from bitterness and heartache and that yoke of despair."

Despair.

She'd felt a sense of desperation and despair for as
long as she could remember. She'd become so cynical and
jaded that she'd stopped making the effort to understand
what being a Christian could mean. And she'd given up
on one of the most important things in life.

Love.

She'd given up on love.

"Maybe it's time to make that next move," she said,
getting up to reach for the journal she'd been avoiding
for days.

Rory waited for her to sit back down. "Are you sure
you want to do this with me here? I can take a walk along
the bay, give you some time alone."

"No. If I'm supposed to forgive her, I'll need you with
me to remind me of that."

"You know that, in your heart."

"But my head is a tad too stubborn to follow that notion."

"That's the thing about humans. We think we have all the answers."

She swallowed the rising fear tearing through her throat. "Okay, I need to get this over and done so I can get on with my life."

Rory gave her a quick kiss. "You can do this, Vanessa. You're strong and you're a fighter."

Vanessa opened the worn journal and took a deep breath.

Soon, she was immersed in baby pictures of herself and several pictures of her mother with various men. Some that Vanessa remembered and others that she'd just as soon forget.

Each picture was dated and marked with captions.

Vanessa's first birthday! We survived even after her daddy walked away. He offered to help me make ends meet, but I told him to never come back if he couldn't come back to stay.

"I don't remember him," Vanessa said, shock jarring her memories into action. "I don't remember having a daddy."

Rory studied the photo. "You were young, a baby still. How could you remember?"

Vanessa went back to searching through the journal.

Vanessa's first day of kindergarten. I hope she'll be okay.

And then, two months later:

We had to move again. Got evicted from that cute little apartment on the beach. I have to find another job. I'm no good at cleaning condos.

"Do you remember any of that?" Rory asked after she'd read the captions out loud.

"Some of it," Vanessa admitted. "This is bringing it all back. I remember a man with dark hair coming to see us right after I started first grade in…what was that little town?" She stopped and stared at her smiling, snaggle-toothed image. "Somewhere in Alabama. I can't remember."

Rory encouraged her. "What happened? Do you remember anything the man did or said?"

"No. Not really." She closed her eyes, the image of her mother sitting out on a porch crying drifting through her memories. "She cried after he left."

Now Vanessa needed to see every page in the little scrapbook. She pored over each and every caption and touched her hand to some of the faded photographs. A few of her mother marrying again, always smiling that hopeful, determined smile. Always looking for love. Searching. Always searching.

In between husbands and a history of Vanessa's childhood, her mother talked about her artwork and how she needed to make a living at it. She wrote about art shows and selling her work to all kinds of customers, from rich, eccentric donors to poor but interested individuals.

Vanessa began to see a pattern here. Her mother had met three of her four husbands at these events. Vanessa couldn't remember how Cora had met Richard.

"A lot of this is about you," Rory said, drawing her back to the journal. "In spite of everything, she treasured these memories of you."

Vanessa pushed at her hair and took a calming breath. "I never knew she kept all of these photos and other things."

Her school pictures. New shoes. A good report card.

Walking on the beach and finding seashells. Lying on the floor, on her stomach, reading a book. Her first teen-aged dance. Wearing vintage clothes.

"I remember being bored at the art shows. I'd go shopping on my own. No wonder I love vintage things so much. I was raised in flea markets and art colonies."

Rory grinned and punched her on the arm. "Well, you always look pretty to me, and you have a good thing going with Vanessa's Vintage, so that's something."

"Yes, that's something."

And then:

I got married again today. He's a preacher! Can you imagine that? But he's so sweet and so kind to me and he buys me pretty things.

Vanessa stared at the photo of her mother with Gregory Pardue. Cora wore a cream-colored suit, and he wore a dark jacket and light-colored pants.

She put the journal down, her stomach churning. "I remember the wedding. I cried because I knew he wasn't a good man. I was afraid of him from the beginning."

"Your instincts were right," Rory said. "But you were too afraid to say anything to anyone."

"I wanted this one to work," she replied. "I so wanted to have a good father, someone who'd take care of us so we could live in a decent house and so I wouldn't have to buy secondhand clothes all the time. By the time they got married, she'd already bought this house, but it needed a lot of work. Later…when she married Richard, he had the whole house redone, and he paid off her mortgage."

"So Richard was the kind of father figure you always wanted."

"Yes." Vanessa held the journal close, her gaze stuck on her mother holding Gregory Pardue's hand. She couldn't stop the shivers moving down her backbone. "I don't remember why she and Gregory broke up. I saw her crying and him packing a suitcase and storming out the door."

"Is that his name? Gregory Pardue?"

"Yes. You don't know him, do you?"

"No. I needed to put a name with the face. In case I do ever run into him."

"I don't think you will. He left the state of Florida, last I heard."

She put the journal down. "I can't read any more right now. But I think I can finish it now. I've moved past the worst part."

"Does it help, knowing your mother did love you? Most of this journal revolves around you, Vanessa. That has to mean something to you."

"It does," she said. "It helps." She got up and moved around the room, that nervous feeling hitting her in the stomach. "I should go and get back to setting up for the estate sale."

Rory started gathering their dishes and the half-eaten food. "I need to get back, too." Drying his hands on a towel, he turned to her. "Are you okay? I mean, do you need me to stay with you at your house for the rest of the day?"

"No. I'm much better now. I don't know what I was so afraid of. I should have read this journal when I first found it."

"It could help you finish what you started," Rory said.

She helped him clean up, relief washing over her. "Remembering things wasn't so bad. Good in places. Sad in others."

But she had a feeling the end would be the worst. Her mother being all alone for the first time in her life. She'd have to deal with that later.

They were headed out the door when she turned to Rory. "Hey, you aren't getting off so easily. You promised you'd share with me, Rory. Or are you stalling out on me again?"

He locked the door and turned to stare over at her. The morning had changed into afternoon. The sun glistened off the water in shades of aqua and sky blue. Birds were chirping in the nearby pines and oaks. Out in the shallows, a brown pelican perched on an old stump with an unmoving calm.

"I was married once," Rory said on a low, calm note.

She turned so quickly to stare over at him the pelican lifted its vast wings and took flight. "What?"

"It's true." He studied the water, his expression etched with sadness. "I knew early on that I wanted to be involved in the church in some sort of capacity. So I went to seminary and while I was there, I met a girl. And we fell in love and got married."

Shock rocketed through Vanessa, burning her with curiosity. "But...what happened?"

Did he get a divorce? Or worse? "Rory?"

"We'd been married for about six months when she got sick," he said. "It was sudden. An aneurysm in her brain. She woke up with a headache one morning and she died that night, in the hospital. She was twenty-four."

Vanessa took in a breath and held both hands to her face so she could keep from sobbing again. "Rory..."

"I know. It's awful. It was awful. We lived in Texas, near the college campus. She was studying to be a nurse, and I was preparing to move us back here so I could begin my ministry. She was six weeks pregnant with our child."

Vanessa sank into the nearest chair. She couldn't speak, couldn't imagine what he'd been through. She reached out a hand to him, but he wasn't looking at her. He was there, back in the past, remembering, reliving.

"I buried her…them…and then I graduated and took on my first assignment, a small country church about fifty miles east of here. I had nowhere to go, but I wasn't really ready to be a minister. I couldn't preach. I wanted to be buried there with them safe in my arms."

Vanessa started crying again, but this time her tears were silent. She got up and went to him and took him in her arms.

Rory didn't say anything. He held her there for a long time, his arms tight around her, his breath moving over her hair and her skin.

"What can I say?" she asked, her fingers stroking his jawline. "What can I do?"

"There is nothing to say or do," he finally managed to say, his words husky and low. "I've heard it all. They're in a better place. It was their time to go. God needed some new angels in Heaven. God has a plan for you, Rory. There's a reason for everything." His eyes burned a deep blue. "I never could figure out the reason for their deaths, however."

Vanessa stood back, her hand stilling on his face, her eyes holding his. "How did you ever come back from that to become the man you are today?"

His eyes, so bright with memories and grief, held her. "I told you. I went to war."

She could understand him so much better now. He'd been angry, and with good reason. "You didn't go over there to fight, did you?"

He nodded his head. "Yes, I thought I'd fight or that maybe I'd get killed. But I was drifting. I'd been assigned to a small church here in Florida, but my heart wasn't in it. I talked to a counselor, a retired minister, and she actually suggested I consider serving as an army chaplain. She'd been through it." He gave Vanessa a weak smile. "So I read up on what it would take, and I did something very impulsive. I joined up and told the recruiters I wanted to go through the Chaplain Candidate Program."

"You became a soldier?"

"Yes, a soldier of sorts. I didn't carry a weapon, but I had a protection detail with me at all times. I went into it hoping to find my soul again. Instead, I found death and heartache and wounded, suffering people. The anger left me when I started talking to the men and women who were serving over there and when I truly started praying for guidance. I guess you could say I had an epiphany. Their pain gave me a reason to live, to help others who were suffering worse than I ever had."

His eyes met hers, holding the trace of darkness she'd sensed when they'd first met. "I realized I wanted to live. And I wanted to help others to live. Men and women who'd seen the worst and suffered the worst. I counseled them and prayed for them and found my calling again. One dark night after a horrible battle, after I'd held the hands of too many dying men, I promised God that if He'd give me the strength to help and serve others, I'd try to lead a happy, content life serving Him."

Vanessa lifted on her toes and kissed Rory, her heart opening and lifting in a way that reminded her of that pelican taking flight. And she finally accepted that she might be falling in love with a man of God.

Chapter Seventeen

The next night, Vanessa checked her reflection in the mirror by the front door, hoping her outfit was suitable for dinner at the Peppermons' house. She wore jeans and a white T-shirt with a bright green fringed scarf around her neck. Wanda had insisted she didn't have to bring anything food-wise. But she had brought a gift for Kandi—some black rose earrings and a long chain necklace. Goth looking but not too far out there.

Vanessa thought about Rory. They'd held each other and talked for a long time, there on the big porch of the camp house.

"I never dreamed you'd been through something so sad, so tragic," she told him. "You're a living example of God's love, Rory."

"It took me a long time to get here," he explained. "And even now, I still have bad days or moments where I sit down and cry. I'll always miss them. I'll always wonder what our child would have been like. But God has blessed me in so many ways. And He gave me the gifts of compassion and understanding."

"You understood me right away," she said. "You saw the pain in my soul."

And now that she could see his pain, she appreciated him even more. They'd made plans to have dinner together on Friday night, after the rummage and estate sales on Friday. Then Blain and Rikki's wedding on Sunday. Rory had asked her to come as his date.

"The minister gets to bring a date?"

"This one does, and he wants her to be you. Or you to be her. Just be there."

So she'd agreed.

They'd taken a new turn in their relationship.

But tonight, she'd made a commitment to be here with Kandi.

The Peppermons lived on the other side of the lake and down a side street that had a partial view of the water. Vanessa followed the directions Wanda had given her and soon saw the big, wood-framed house that Wanda had described.

The house was painted a deep blue, with white shutters and porch railings. Several white rocking chairs lined both sides of the wide front door. Hanging baskets with red geraniums and pink-and-white petunias swayed at each corner of the long porch. The yard was also full of flower beds, mulched and overflowing with blossoms and plants of every size and color.

Vanessa thought that if she lived here, she'd never want to leave. She walked up the steps to the big door and pressed the doorbell, nerves ringing in her head right along with the bell that loudly played Beethoven's "Ode to Joy."

Then she heard the pounding of several feet thundering throughout the house, followed by shouting.

The door tore open and a young boy with pecan-colored skin grinned up at her. "I got it," he called over his shoulder. "It's Kandi's friend, Van-Esther."

Vanessa smiled at the mispronunciation of her name. "Hi," she said, unsure what to do next. A full house scared her a lot more than an empty one.

"Hi," he said, tugging her inside the wide hallway of the house. "I'm Derek."

"Hello, Derek," Vanessa replied, the whirl of a ceiling fan cooling the cold sweat sticking to her backbone. Why was she so terrified of children? It wasn't that she was afraid of kids. She loved them. But she had a fear of doing or saying the wrong thing around them. What if she did that with Kandi?

A vision of Rory holding a baby planted itself inside her head and caused her to sweat even more.

"Hi, come on back," Wanda called, her head peeking out from what had to be the kitchen on one side of the long hallway.

Derek reached for Vanessa's hand. "We're having the best dinner. Taco salad."

"I love taco salad," Vanessa said, wondering how Wanda and Carl managed to feed so many mouths. She'd seen kids hanging out in rooms on both sides of the hallway, some reading and studying and others watching television. But she hadn't spotted Kandi yet.

Derek guided her to the right side of the house where a country kitchen ran into a big dining room, both rooms spacious and bright and spick-and-span clean.

"Welcome," Wanda said from her spot in front of the stove. She stirred a huge pot of taco meat with one hand while one of the younger children hung away from the stove's heat on her hip.

"Find a seat. It's about ready." She lifted her chin toward the stairs. "Kandi is cleaning her room. She'll be down soon."

"Okay."

Vanessa smiled at Wanda, noting her clipped salt-and-pepper hair and her chunky, solid frame. She wore old jeans and a faded yellow shirt underneath a white apron splotched with all colors of paint that said *We are all God's children*.

Vanessa decided she *would* stay here forever. Who would ever notice her anyway? She'd merge into the crowd of children of all ages and colors that moved at random through the many rooms of the house. The energy was magnetic and endearing.

Then the back door opened and Carl walked in, wearing work clothes. His shirt pocket was embroidered with the title of Millbrook Gardens Nursery and Landscaping.

That explained the lovely front yard and the many hanging baskets. She could imagine Wanda and Carl puttering around in the garden with a string of kids following them.

"Hi," he said, waving to Vanessa. Then he kissed Wanda and took the giggling toddler off her hip. "Hey, honey, you got room for one more tonight?"

Wanda laughed out loud. "Sure. We'll add another taco shell or two to the twenty-four we already have. Who'd you invite to dinner this time?"

Carl walked back to the door and motioned. "Oh, just the preacher. He was walking along the lake like he'd lost his best friend."

And in walked Rory, bearing a sheepish smile. When he looked up at Vanessa, he shrugged. "I told him I was fine, but he insisted I hop in and come home with him."

Remembering their intimate conversation yesterday, she felt as shy and unsteady as he looked. And yet she was so glad to see him. "Hi."

She wanted to run to him and hold him close, but she'd settle for having him nearby for now. When they'd parted late yesterday afternoon, Vanessa had accepted that she was in love with Rory. She wasn't sure what to do about that.

She felt a strong sense of relief at seeing him. He'd help guide her through this maze of children and keep her from saying or doing the wrong thing. Probably in the same way he'd helped her since the first time she'd laid eyes on him.

But Vanessa also now knew *he* wasn't always fine. He probably enjoyed these gatherings more than anyone because he loved people and he was so good with children. She smiled to reassure him, then got up and decided to get busy. "Wanda, what can I do to help?"

Wanda stirred meat and barked orders. "We all have jobs around here. If anything is left over after everyone does their assigned task, I guess you can get out that other box of taco shells and stick 'em in the oven."

Vanessa motioned to Rory. "Don't think you're gonna get away with doing nothing."

Rory appeared relieved and hurried toward Vanessa. Together they raided the big pantry that Wanda pointed to while she issued orders all around. Rory winked at Vanessa and whispered, "I didn't plan this, but I've wanted to see you all day long. How are you?"

"Good, now that you're here," she replied. "How about you?"

"I'm great. I feel lighthearted and…free."

Vanessa could relate to that feeling. "Me, too. I guess confession *is* good for the soul."

"You can say that again. You're good for my soul."

"I'm going to get cleaned up," Carl called over the chaos. "That way I get out of being bossed around."

"You have cleanup duty in here later, too," Wanda called.

Vanessa's heart filled with something so foreign and sweet, she had to stop and watch the confusion in order to figure it out.

Joy. She felt a great rush of joy.

No wonder Wanda wore that apron.

Rory saw her expression, his gaze holding hers. "They are amazing, aren't they?"

She nodded. "Yes, they are." Then she turned to him. "I'm glad you're here."

He took the bag of taco shells and grinned over at her. "I didn't want you to think I'd wormed my way in on this dinner so I could see you. But that is an added bonus."

She shrugged. "Carl invited you, so you had to accept."

"Yes, but I accepted two seconds quicker when I remembered you'd be here."

"I'm doubly glad now. I need you for moral support."

"You're scared?"

"Completely," she said. "I don't think I'd be a good mother. I wouldn't know how to handle any of this, let alone a crying baby or confused teen."

He passed her the tacos to put on a baking sheet. "You keep saying that, but I think you'd make a great mother."

Vanessa stared over at him, wishing she felt the same way. Then it occurred to her that Rory had almost been a father. He'd lost the baby his wife was carrying, along with her.

If he ever found the right woman, he'd want more children.

But as much as it hurt her even to think such a thing, Vanessa wasn't sure she was the motherly type. She hadn't had a very good role model. And that meant she and Rory might not have a future together after all.

* * *

Rory enjoyed watching Vanessa as she got to know the kids. Kandi and Vanessa were in the kitchen, cutting and serving brownies and ice cream. They talked and laughed as if they were old friends. Kandi could either help Vanessa get over her fear of motherhood or cause her to stand firm on never having children.

He prayed both of them would find some sort of encouragement by being around each other. He thought of yesterday and how he and Vanessa had held each other and kissed after they'd both opened old wounds. His heart bumped faster each time he thought about their time together.

The old guilt pushed at him, making him wonder if he could take that final step toward finding his soul mate. Was Vanessa that woman, the one who could finally fill that hole that ran deep inside his heart? He believed it and he prayed about it.

He wanted her in his life.

"You look awfully pensive," Carl said as he handed Rory a bowl full of vanilla ice cream mixed with brownie chunks. "Troubles, Preacher?"

Rory grinned and shook his head. "No, not really. Trouble, but in a good way, I think."

"The way you keep staring at Vanessa, I think I know that kind of trouble, my friend. And I've been married to her for close to thirty years."

Rory took a bite of the vanilla ice cream and chased it with a chunk of moist brownie. The brain freeze almost jarred him out of his musings. "I think I might be ready for the challenge," he admitted, knowing Carl wouldn't repeat his words, except maybe to Wanda. "We'll have to see what happens."

"Do you want her in your life?" Carl asked on a low chuckle. "Are you ready for everything that involves?"

"I think so. The problem is convincing her that she's the one for me. Her confidence level needs boosting. She thinks she's not good wife-mother-marriage material."

Carl shook his head and laughed and then grabbed up a four-year-old little girl and gave her a big hug. The child smiled shyly at Rory and pointed a chubby finger. "Peacher."

"That is the peacher, Betsy," Carl said without correcting her. "He's a good guy."

"Good," Betsy said, smiling at Rory.

He grinned back and tickled at her shoulder. "Where's your ice cream?"

She wiggled out of Carl's embrace. "More," she said in a singsong voice as she headed back to the kitchen.

Kandi scooped her up and sat her on the counter. "Here's yours, Betsy-bell."

Rory imagined Vanessa with a child, his heart burning with an intense need. "Kandi seems happier than I've seen her in a while."

"She's doing better," Carl admitted. "Her grades have come up and she's helping out more around here. Wanda and she have lots of late-night talks."

"Vanessa really wants to be a good mentor to her," Rory said. "She's been through a lot herself."

Carl studied the action in the kitchen. "We've all got something, don't we?"

Rory nodded and finished his dessert. "Thanks for asking me over, Carl. And thanks for the pep talk. I'm a little rusty in the 'figuring out a woman' department."

Carl slapped a meaty hand across Rory's back. "I hate to break it to you, Preacher. But there ain't no such thing as figuring out a woman."

Rory laughed and lifted his spoon in the air. "I do believe you're correct on that matter."

When he glanced back to the kitchen, Vanessa smiled at him.

"And Kandi wants to go to college to study fashion design. She's an artist, too. She showed me some of her sketches. She has a lot of talent."

"So I take it tonight was a success?" Rory asked as they drove along Lake Street. She'd insisted on giving him a ride home, and he hadn't argued with that notion.

"Yes. She was like a different person. She laughed and talked and I felt as if we really connected—" She stopped and glanced over at him. "I sound so corny, don't I?"

"You sound happy," Rory said. "You sound as if you were born to be a positive role model."

"Not born to it," she quickly corrected. "But hopeful, Rory. I hope I'll make a difference in Kandi's life. She opened up a little about how her mother had died, and it broke my heart. I know she's been through all kinds of things, but she can't tell me everything." Vanessa pulled into the driveway of her house. "She goes to a therapist. She did tell me that much."

Rory turned so he could see Vanessa's face. "Did you ever go through therapy?"

"No. I buried it all deep inside. You're the first person I've ever told the whole truth."

Rory wondered how Miss Fanny had found out and decided maybe Vanessa's mother had confessed to her friend in a final attempt to find some peace before she died. Why hadn't she made an attempt to ask Vanessa to forgive her?

"I'm okay, Rory," she said. Then she shook her head.

"I have issues. A lot of issues. But I'm working through them with each room in this house."

"Do you sleep in that bedroom?" he asked.

She went still, her eyes on the house. "I sleep on the couch in the den most nights."

"All the time," he amended. Then he reached for her and tugged her close. "You're not alone, Vanessa. I want you to always remember that."

"I will," she said against his chest. Then she lifted away and opened the car door.

Rory got out and stood watching her.

She turned at the steps. "Want to come in for coffee or a soda?"

"I thought you'd never ask," he said.

He didn't want her to be alone tonight. At least this way, he could stay with her for a little while before he had to go home. But it also occurred to him that accepting her invitation to come in for coffee worked out for him, too.

Because he didn't want to be alone anymore either.

Chapter Eighteen

Wanda had sent brownies home with them, so Rory watched as Vanessa made coffee and got a plate.

"I shouldn't eat another one," she said, bringing the plate to the living room coffee table. "But they're so good."

"She makes them from scratch," Rory said. He helped pour the coffee and followed her into the living room. "We can walk this off or go kayaking again. But I think working the sales on Friday will take care of burning off a lot of calories."

Vanessa seemed pensive, her emotions close to the surface. "It's really going to happen, isn't it?"

"Are you ready for this?" he asked. "I did push you into holding your sale in conjunction with ours. Maybe I should have let you handle things on your own."

"No. I'm glad you forced the issue." She lifted her hand in the air. "I'd still be sitting in the middle of the floor trying to sort through all of this. I needed a firm deadline." Then she shrugged. "I need to get this part of my life over and done with."

Rory wondered what she would do with her life once this place was out of her system.

After they'd settled onto the old couch, he glanced around. "I like this house."

"It'll be for sale soon. Make me an offer."

He'd buy it in a heartbeat. But only if she'd come with it. "That's tempting. You're tempting."

She smiled at that. "Is this brownie tempting?"

"Yes." He grabbed the last one and held it away from her. Then he fed it to her, piece by piece, thinking he could get used to nights such as this. Nights with her.

"So where will that leave us?" he asked, hoping he wouldn't break the tender understanding they had between them now. "What happens after you sell this house?"

"I don't know." She put down her coffee and stared out onto the big sunporch. "I never planned to stay here."

"And I never planned to ask you to stay here."

Her eyes glistened with hope and confusion. "Are you? Asking me to stay?"

"I can't make you stay but…I want you to stay."

She gave him a sweet smile, but her eyes still held that trace of hesitancy and doubt. "I have my boutique and my website to consider."

"And I have no right to tell you what to do about either of those. You're a businesswoman. You have obligations."

Which didn't include him. So where did that leave them?

"I can visit—a lot."

"Not if you sell the house. You wouldn't have any reason to come back here."

"You'd be my reason, Rory. I mean, if you want to be my reason. If you want me to come back. And you can come and see me in New Orleans."

"So we'd have this back-and-forth, long-distance type relationship?"

"Yes. I could stay with Marla and Alec. Or in a hotel out on the bay."

He wanted more, but he couldn't ask for more. This was all so new and different. "We probably need to think about things and consider what we're saying here."

Vanessa nodded, but he saw a trace of disappointment in her eyes. "You know how hard I fought this. I'm not the typical starry-eyed woman looking for love."

He'd certainly seen that from the first. "You have a lot of love to give." He had to ask. "Don't take this the wrong way. We're still…getting to know each other, but these are things I have to ask. Is the having-a-family thing holding you back? You really don't want to have children? Or is it me? Maybe you like me but you don't want to have a relationship with a minister."

She stared over at him with those big eyes. "You have a right to know the answers to those questions. I just don't know the answers. I'm still afraid I'll mess it all up—marriage and a family. You. I'd rather keep you as a friend than lose you because I make the wrong move."

Rory pulled her close. "You will never lose me. Ever. No matter what."

And he prayed he wouldn't lose her.

Vanessa leaned over and kissed him. "I can't believe how I feel, Rory. It's so…rich. I feel full and rich, and my heart is doing a funny dance. I—"

Her cell rang. And then Rory's cell rang.

"It's Wanda," she said, glancing at Rory.

"And Carl," he said. "This can't be good."

He answered Carl's call while she did the same with Wanda.

"Kandi is missing," Carl said. "We went up for bed check, and she'd stuffed her mattress with pillows and clothes. But she's gone."

"I'll be right there," Rory said. Then he stood and watched Vanessa's face.

"We're on our way," she said. She ended the call and rushed into his arms. "They think she's with the Goth guy."

"Let's go," Rory said. He needed to call in reinforcements. Blain would help. "I'll call Blain on the way."

"We have to find her," Vanessa said. "She was so happy tonight. She seemed like a different person. We talked and laughed, and she was so pleasant."

"That's because she knew she would be leaving after dinner to meet up with him," Rory said. "They've probably been planning this for weeks."

"I should have paid more attention," Vanessa told him. "I worried that she'd been through a lot of what I went through."

"Not that I know of," Rory replied. "But she might have been pushed around by other boyfriends. She spent a lot of time out there on her own growing up."

They made it to the Peppermons' house in record time.

When they pulled up, all of the lights were on and a patrol car was parked in the yard. So was Blain's pickup truck. Blain must have put the pedal to the metal, too.

Rory and Vanessa rushed toward the house, but he pulled her close before they got inside. "We have to stay cool and positive, for their sake, okay?"

Vanessa nodded. "Rory, should we pray?"

Touched that she wanted that, he nodded and pulled her into his arms. Then he whispered an urgent prayer as they held each other there. "Help us to find this confused young girl, Lord."

Vanessa held tight to him and then stood back. "I'm ready. Let's go inside."

* * *

"We're doing everything we can to find her," Blain told the Peppermons. "She can't get far since you discovered her missing a little while ago."

Vanessa sat holding one of the younger children who'd woken in the middle of all the chaos. Her heart hurt for this loving family and for Kandi. Maybe this boy was okay and truly cared about her, or maybe he only wanted to seduce her and hurt her.

I need You, Lord.

Vanessa kissed the little girl's reddish-blond hair. Emma. Little Emma. She now knew the names of all the children who lived in this house.

And she wasn't afraid of them anymore. Instead, she wanted to cuddle each of them and fight for them and protect them from that big, scary world out there. Why had she ever worried that her heart couldn't love? Right now, her heart ached with love.

Then realization filled her mind. It was the *love* she was so afraid of. This kind of love that took your breath away and held your soul in a tender capture. This fierce, protective love that made you want to harm anyone who dared hurt a child.

Had her mother felt that way at times?

She'd have to finish reading that journal.

She listened to Blain's soft, steady voice. He'd gone over every detail. Where did the boy—Jerome "Rocky" Asher—live? How old was he? How had they met? Did they hang out at school?

Jerome lived on the other side of town, and they'd met at an ice-cream stand out on the beach. He had dropped out of school and hung with an older crowd known for drug use and vagrancy.

The worst possible scenario. What if he'd taken her somewhere and enticed her to use drugs?

Wanda came over to Vanessa. "Do you need anything?"

"I should be asking you that," Vanessa said. "I wish I could do more."

"You're here and that counts." Wanda took Emma. "I'm going to get her back to bed. You can man the drink counters. I have snacks in the pantry."

Vanessa gladly took over kitchen duty. She made coffee and sliced homemade banana bread. Soon, several people from the church and the foster-parent support group showed up. Vanessa listened and watched and got everyone something to eat or drink. It was going to be a long night.

She watched Rory. He made sure everyone got prayed over or prayed with or prayed for. She loved him. She knew that in her heart right now, and she also knew that she couldn't leave him.

But she'd have to make some tough decisions about staying here. In this town, married to a preacher.

What do you think about that, Mom?

"How you doing?" Rory asked, his fingers tangling with hers after he'd walked up close.

"I'm okay. It's hard to breathe, but I'm doing what you said. I have to be strong for them. I love this family."

"We all do."

He gave her a quick kiss. "You should rest."

"I can't. Do you want something to eat or drink?"

"I'm fine."

He stood with her in the kitchen, waiting. The agony of not knowing, of imagining the worst, or hoping for the best, made Vanessa want to throw something.

But Rory's hand in hers held her there, steadying her like an anchor holding a lost ship.

"Is this how it feels?" she asked him. "Is this how God holds us when we're scared and out of options? The same way you're holding me now?"

"Yes."

"I'm beginning to get it, Rory. I need Him in my life. I could never get through this night without Him. Or you."

"We're here, both of us," Rory said. "Hang tight."

Vanessa heard her phone ringing. Searching on the counter for her purse, she dug inside.

"It's Kandi," she told Rory.

Rory immediately called out to Blain and the Peppermons.

"Hello?" Vanessa said, trying to keep her voice calm.

"I need help."

"Where are you?"

"In the park by the bay, underneath the white gazebo. Vanessa, come alone, please."

"I'm on my way."

She ended the call and told Rory and the others what Kandi had said. "I'm going. I have to."

Blain nodded. "Okay, but you won't really be alone. I'm going to follow you and park my truck on the other end of the park. I'll walk it the rest of the way and stay in the trees."

"I'm going with you, Blain," Rory said.

Blain didn't argue. "Let's go then."

"We'll call you," Blain told Wanda. "Meantime, stay here and if she calls again, just assure her that Vanessa is on the way. Alone."

Vanessa grabbed her purse and went to her car, glad they'd brought her car to save time earlier.

"Be careful," Rory said. "It could be a setup."

"I'll be fine," Vanessa said. But she was glad to know Blain and Rory would be nearby.

And that the Lord would watch over Kandi and Vanessa, too.

Chapter Nineteen

The Bayside Park was dark and deserted this late at night. With one road forming a horseshoe that circled in and out, and dense shrubs and trees all around, it could be beautiful by day and dangerous by night.

Vanessa hadn't been here in over ten years. But she knew exactly why Kandi would come here with a boy. It was secluded and shadowy. Private. Too private.

Vanessa pulled her tiny car up into the gravel parking space and cut the engine. The white gazebo sat in the middle of the open area by the water, glowing eerily in the moonlight.

Taking a calming breath, she got out and started walking up the dirt lane to the water. "Kandi?"

"I'm here."

Vanessa followed the sound of the girl's shaky voice. And then she saw a dark figure huddled on the round table inside the wide gazebo. Hurrying now, she rushed up to Kandi's side.

"Are you all right?"

Kandi looked up, and Vanessa saw the fear and shame on the girl's face. And the swollen right eye. "What happened?"

"He…he didn't like the word no," Kandi said through a sob.

Vanessa felt sick to her stomach. "Did he…?"

"No." Kandi shook her head and wiped at her eyes. "It got ugly but I'm okay."

"Where is he?" Vanessa asked, hoping Blain and Rory would take care of finding Jerome.

"He took off through the park after we fought. I told him I was going to call the police."

"Smart girl."

"Not so smart," Kandi retorted. "He had me fooled, you know. Said I was the one for him. That he could take away all my troubles." She gulped in a sob. "Then later he told me he'd come back and finish the job if I ratted him out."

"He won't," Vanessa said. "The police will find him."

"I should have known he was a loser," Kandi said. "But he treated me so good at first."

Terrible memories whispered around Vanessa, making her shiver in the warm wind. Gregory Pardue had been sweet and generous to her mother and to Vanessa, too, at first. Pushing the dark thoughts away, she asked, "Did he…try to give you drugs?"

"Of course," Kandi said. "And I almost let him." She wrapped her arms against her ribs. "He told me I'd feel good, that all of my troubles would disappear. But I thought of Miss Wanda and Mr. Carl and how much they'd done for me, even when I was so mean and ugly toward them. And I thought of my mom and how drugs and alcohol had killed her."

Vanessa kept her hand on Kandi's arm but didn't speak. Emotion clogged her throat, but she had to keep it together.

"It was almost as if my mom was standing here, telling me to stop. Telling me to run away. When I was little, she used to tell me that I was special. That I'd be okay, no matter what. I had this image of her in my head, and that's when I told him no."

"She's watching over you," Vanessa said in a quiet voice.

A tear moved down her right cheek, an image of her mother whispering sweet words in her ear. *You'll be okay, honey. One day, your daddy will come for us.*

How could she have forgotten that? And how could she love someone so much and still resent that same person for her past troubles? It all stemmed from needing to know the truth, from needing proof. But faith was the substance of things not seen...

Vanessa wished that day her mother had promised her had come, but she understood a lot now about what being a parent involved. Kandi and the Peppermons had taught her that. Rory had talked to her about family, too. Marla had shown her what a real family could be like. Miss Fanny had been family to Cora.

"Why did you call me?" she asked Kandi. "Why not Wanda or Carl?"

Kandi shrugged and sniffed, her cheeks shadowed with smeared mascara and eyeliner. "Because you're like me," she said. "You lost your mother, and you never mention having a daddy either. And you were afraid to go inside that church the first night we met."

"Yes, all of that is true," Vanessa said. "You've got me pegged."

Kandi looked out toward the woods. "I trust you."

Vanessa's heart fell open, but instead of hurting, the old wounds tingled with a new awareness, a sort of healing. "I'm glad you called me."

"I'm in a lot of trouble," Kandi said. "I don't know how to get out of this mess. This life."

"You will be okay," Vanessa said. "You used your head, and you stopped this before it became too late."

"But what if it's too late for me anyway?" Kandi asked, tears streaming down her face.

"It's never too late for you to turn your life around," Vanessa replied, hearing the words herself. She needed to remember that. "You've got good people in your life, people who are willing to help you and love you. Let's get you home."

Kandi got up and pulled at her torn clothes. "Are they mad at me?"

"They're worried," Vanessa said. "But as soon as I call them, they'll be relieved, too."

After she'd phoned Wanda and told her she was bringing Kandi home, Vanessa called Rory. "We're on our way."

"I know," he said. "You were great with her."

Vanessa breathed a sigh of relief, knowing Rory and Blain had been there in the shadows. "She's the one who helped me, Rory."

"Blain has put out the word on Jerome Asher. He'll be brought in for questioning on several counts, and if we find drugs on him, he'll be in a lot of trouble. But it'll be up to the Peppermons and their caseworker on how to handle this situation. Or whether or not they'll press charges."

Vanessa glanced over at Kandi. The girl leaned against the window, her eyes closed. "You know what I think should be done."

"I'm getting the picture, yes. And I tend to agree with you. Get her home and we'll talk."

At around two in the morning, Vanessa pulled up to

the Peppermon house. Now that everyone knew Kandi was safe, most of the people who'd come to help had left. Probably best since the girl was exhausted, embarrassed and in no mood for prying eyes.

"Let's get you inside," Vanessa said.

She guided Kandi up the steps, but the front door burst open before they could reach it.

Wanda opened her arms, tears misting in her eyes.

Kandi ran to her and held her tight. "I'm sorry, Miss Wanda."

"Shhh," Wanda said. "It's okay. We'll talk tomorrow. Right now, let's get you a nice bath so you can sleep." She looked at Vanessa over the girl's head, her eyes wide with the one question.

Vanessa shook her head and mouthed, "She's okay."

The look of relief in Wanda's eyes mirrored the relief Vanessa felt in her soul. She'd avoided a similar incident when she'd been Kandi's age. Another shiver moved down her spine. She was so thankful the girl had managed to get herself out of a bad situation, too.

Thank You, God.

After Wanda gave Kandi some water and crackers and took her upstairs, Vanessa stood in the kitchen and stared out the window. The darkness swirled with memories and pain, a sort of frustration that she couldn't shake.

When she felt a hand on her shoulder, she turned to find Rory standing there. He took her into his arms and held her close, his lips touching her temple.

Vanessa took one long breath, and then she burst into tears.

An hour later, Rory and Vanessa made it back to her house.

"I'm exhausted," she said, her voice raspy. "I'm sure you are, too."

"Yep." He felt the weight of the night pushing against his shoulders. "I hope Blain hauls Jerome in and gives him a few good reasons to leave Kandi alone."

"I hope he sends him to jail," Vanessa said, a bitterness edging her words.

"This brought it all back, didn't it?"

He'd seen the way she kept staring out the window. How she held herself, her arms in a protective shield against her body.

"Yes." She turned to him, her expression grim. "Jerome is younger and more edgy, but it's the same. Gaining her trust, telling her what she wants to hear, promising her something better. I heard all of that from Gregory. My mom heard all of that, too. I never thought about it until tonight, but that man tricked both of us."

"He was evil, Vanessa. And he was working to put a wedge between you and your mother."

"Well, it worked," she said. "I let him do that to us. She let him do that to me."

"You can let go of all of that now."

"Can I?" she asked. "I thought I could. But tonight, it all came tumbling back."

Rory didn't know how to reach her, and he worried that she would slip away again. "You helped a young girl, Vanessa. You helped her *because* of what you've been through and in spite of it, too. Look at the blessing in that…and be thankful that you were able to get through to Kandi enough that she trusted you to call you."

Vanessa leaned against the kitchen counter and stared over at him. "It's late and we're both tired. We have a busy week, starting tomorrow."

"I guess that's my cue to go," Rory said, wishing he could stay. But they did have lots to do before the big event on Friday. And they still had work to do before they'd be free and clear of their past hang-ups.

He turned to leave, a heaviness centered in his heart.

"Rory?"

He whirled around. "Yes?"

"I'm sorry. You're right. I've still got a long way to go before I feel secure in this new skin. But I did turn to God tonight. I did pray for Him to help us. I need to accept that He's with me—all the time. Even at the worst of times."

"I'm glad about that," Rory said. "And I believe He hears our prayers even if He doesn't answer them in the way we think He should. But I also believe there can be a blessing in everything that happens to us, good or bad. Having faith is all about searching for the blessings. It's about the things we can't see."

"That verse—you talked about it on Easter Sunday. It stayed with me, Rory." She came to him and hugged him close. "I think faith is about the things we can't feel either. The things we long to feel, the things the Lord wants us to feel."

"You're so right on that," he said. Then he kissed her and headed back to his place, thankful that they'd managed to help Kandi and hopeful that the whole experience would help Vanessa, too.

"So I'll see you on Friday, too," Marla told Vanessa the next day. She'd come by to help Vanessa get the last of her items on display. They'd tagged some of the big items and put signs on all of the display tables and surfaces to show the price structure. "You've got some good stuff here, Vanessa. The place is looking good."

"Feel free to shop now," Vanessa told her. "Things might get busy Friday. I'll even throw in some freebies to pay you back all the cupcake donations and to thank you for offering to help me man the checkout table."

"I've only given you a couple of cupcakes," Marla said. But her eyes lit up at the prospect of shopping early. "And I won't be the only volunteer here helping out."

"You've given me more than just cupcakes," Vanessa said. "You're a good friend, Marla."

She'd told Marla about what had happened last night. But the Millbrook Lake grapevine had already taken on the story anyway. And Jerome Asher had been apprehended and brought in for questioning. If nothing else, at least maybe it would scare him into thinking about the consequences of his actions from now on. He was over twenty-one, and even though Kandi had gone with him of her own accord, she was still a minor.

"I'm so glad everything turned out okay with Kandi," Marla said now. "And I'm really glad that you and Rory have grown closer."

Vanessa couldn't deny her feelings for Rory. "He's amazing. He's been patient with me. And he's helped me work through some of my angst."

"Rory is a good man," Marla said, her green eyes bright with hope. "He needs someone to love him."

"I think I do love him," Vanessa admitted. "But I'm afraid to tell him that. I have to be sure."

Marla tried on a straw sun hat. "What's holding you back?"

"I don't know," Vanessa said. "Well, I do know. I live and work in New Orleans. I want to sell this house and get on with my life. This house has become an albatross of sorts, and now that I've inherited all of Richard's holdings, too, I'm not sure what to do with myself."

Marla dropped the hat and picked up a floral cotton scarf. "You're blessed, Vanessa. You don't have to worry about money anymore. And believe me, I know that feeling. I married Alec because I love him so much, but the security of not having to worry about how to pay the bills is nice." She tossed the scarf around her neck and lifted her red-gold hair. "Alec and I don't take any of it for granted. We can help the community and the church, and Alec is happy with his Caldwell Canines training facility."

"You've both found your purpose," Vanessa said. "I'm still searching for mine."

Marla placed the pretty scarf in her growing pile of "to buy" things. "Well, now you can find a purpose. You have the ability to make a difference in the world."

Vanessa glanced over at her mother's journal and wondered if Cora would have been happy with more money and more status. Richard had tried to give her those things, and for the last few years of her life, she'd been content.

Wishing now she'd spent more time with her mother during those happy years, Vanessa told herself she had to get past all the mistakes and failures in her life and start living, really living. With Rory.

"You're right," she said to Marla. "I have an opportunity that few people get. I can do something good in this world. Now I have to figure out what that is."

A knock at the front door caused her to whirl around. "That might be Rory."

Marla grinned. "I need to get out of your hair and get back to the shop."

But when Vanessa opened the door, Kandi was standing there.

"Hi," she said, surprised that the girl was here. "Why aren't you in school?"

"Half day," Kandi said. "Miss Wanda is parking the

car over at the church. She's coming over, too. To help you."

When she saw Marla, Kandi looked embarrassed. "I...I didn't know you had someone in here with you."

"You remember Marla, I'm sure," Vanessa said. "She's the cupcake lady. Marla's Marvelous Desserts."

"Right," Kandi said. "You brought cupcakes from her shop to the youth meeting that first night."

"I sure did," Vanessa said. "They were a hit."

"Good to see you again, Kandi," Marla said. "I've seen you in church a lot, of course."

Kandi nodded and pushed at her always-rumpled hair. "Want me to start in another room, Vanessa?"

"You can help me in here," Vanessa replied, deciding she should keep Kandi close just in case the teen needed to vent some more.

Marla gave Vanessa a questioning glance and then smiled at Kandi. "I'm so glad you're here. I'm always looking for summer help in the bakery, and I was wondering if you might be willing to work a few hours a week. I can only pay minimum wage and I know we'd have to clear things with your foster parents and your caseworker, but will you consider it?"

Kandi stared at Marla for a few seconds, her eyes wide and her expression unsure. Finally, she said, "I could use some spending money." She gave Vanessa one of her kohl-rimmed stares. "I'd already thought about finding a summer job since I'm sixteen now."

"Great," Marla said as she breezed by. "I'll call Wanda and we'll set something up for you to come in and fill out an application."

After Marla headed out the back door, Kandi turned to Vanessa. "Do you think she'll let me work for her?"

"She wouldn't have asked you if she didn't mean it," Vanessa said. "You'd be great at the bakery."

Kandi lifted a red leather purse and toyed with the strap. "Your mom sure had a lot of stuff."

"Yes, she did," Vanessa said. Then she finished sorting through some T-shirts. "How are you?"

Kandi stared at a T-shirt with a dolphin motif on its front. "I'm okay. I stayed home from school yesterday, and then we had only a half day today. People were staring at me. I guess I'll have a reputation now. Even worse than before."

"People are curious," Vanessa replied. "And some of them will be cruel. But you hold your head up and ignore them. They don't know what you've been through, so they shouldn't make speculations. Don't let them get to you."

"Or what? You'll storm the school yard and scare them away?"

"If you need me to do that," Vanessa said. "But I'm thinking you're able to overcome that kind of stuff all on your own."

Kandi's smile wasn't so sure. "What do you need me to do?"

Vanessa dropped the subject and pointed to a box of old books and magazines. "We need to get these in some sort of order. I'll toss the ones that don't have any value and save some for the collectors who'll show up tomorrow. If you can sort them by magazine name, that would help. And put the books on that table over there with the rest of them. And if you find any documents or business papers, put those here on this old desk." She pointed to the old rolltop near the front window.

Kandi went to work with the various magazines, books and old folders. Soon Wanda came in with a platter of snack cake. "I think Rory smelled this spice cake. He might show up over here."

Vanessa nodded. She missed Rory. She hadn't seen much of him yesterday. And she wasn't sure about anything regarding their feelings for each other. "The more the merrier," she said. "I'm so ready to get this house in order."

Chapter Twenty

Rory never made it over on Thursday.

But Friday dawned bright and sunny, with the church parking lot full to capacity and the side streets along the lake lined with vehicles. The rummage sale at the church was in full swing, and Vanessa had a steady stream of people moving through her house.

Her house.

She had to grit her teeth and turn away because she wanted to shout to all of them to leave. She wasn't ready to give up her memories or her pain. Each item she sold tore at her hurting heart like a jagged knife. How could she let go of her mother's possessions by selling them to strangers?

But she would have to let them go. She would because Rory had shown her how Christ had been willing to die for her pain. To save her from any pain. To wash away her sins and make her whole again in a new life.

A new life.

She couldn't wait to see Rory and to tell him how she felt. The pain of letting go was slowly being replaced with the hope of living again. With Christ at the center of her life.

Two hours later, she took a breath and went to the rolltop to look for a notepad. Then she saw a note from Kandi lying there.

Found this in one of the books. I didn't open it.

It was a sealed envelope addressed to Vanessa.

From her mother. She recognized the elaborate handwriting, all scrolls and loops and curlicues. The same kind of handwriting as the verse she'd read on the little plaque she'd found in the kitchen.

"Vanessa, can you help me with this dresser?" one of the volunteers called. "We're haggling on the price," she whispered when Vanessa whirled around.

"I'll be right there," Vanessa said, her mind still on that sealed envelope. But it would have to wait. She had too many people in her house right now to open it anyway.

She'd need to open this in private. So she tucked the envelope into her mother's journal, which she'd placed on the desk before the sale. Then she put the journal back into the cubbyhole inside the open rolltop and pulled the cover back down.

Rory looked around the church gathering room.

They'd had a very successful sale, which had netted a lot of money for the church. That money would go toward their mission work, which included helping the homeless, giving funds to the foster-parent organization and even donating always-needed funding to the new animal rescue shelter that had opened up in town. He glanced across the way, wondering how Vanessa had fared.

He'd gone over a couple times to help move heavy purchases, and they'd spoken briefly but she'd been busy, very busy.

They were supposed to go to dinner tonight. Then she'd be at Blain's wedding on Sunday afternoon, too.

After that, he wasn't sure what would happen, but Rory knew the Lord would show him the way. Always.

"What about all of this?" Barbara asked, her short hair sticking up like tufts of grass while her gaze scanned the leftover items that hadn't sold.

"We'll clean up tomorrow and send a truck full of stuff to the local thrift store," he said. "You go home and rest. You worked hard today."

"And don't my tired feet know it," Barbara retorted. "What about you? You got plans?"

"I do," Rory said. "I'm taking Vanessa out to dinner."

Barbara stared at his feet. "You aren't wearing those flip-flops, are you?"

Rory chuckled. "No. I'm wearing pants—which is good, I think—and a nice shirt. And real shoes."

"Whew, scared me there for a minute."

His secretary, ever the dramatic clown.

After Barbara and the other volunteers left, he glanced back across the street, his heart full and grateful.

He couldn't wait to have a real dinner with Vanessa.

Vanessa checked her reflection in the bedroom mirror. She'd found a gorgeous blue dress in the back of her mother's closet, and she'd had it cleaned for tonight. It had a white portrait collar and a full skirt that flared out around her legs. She wore white strappy sandals with it, and she'd put her hair up in a loose chignon.

She was nervous.

But ready. So ready to have a night with Rory where they didn't need to talk about the big sale or her problems or his administrative duties as a minister. Tonight, she wanted small talk, silly, quirky, fun talk. And maybe a nice walk along the lake, in the moonlight.

She moved through the house, amazed at how big and

empty it felt now that so much of the furniture and clutter had been removed. This old place had good bones. It was spacious and rambling and sunny in places but nice and cool in other places.

She prayed someone would buy it and make it into a showcase again.

Then her gaze hit on the old desk by the window.

And the sealed envelope she'd stuck into one of the cubbyholes.

Checking her watch, she debated whether to open it before Rory came over to pick her up. She had to know in the same way she had to know the rest of the journal's content. She'd waited all day, and then she'd hurried to get a shower, followed by the frenzy of hair and makeup and what shoes to wear with this vivid blue dress.

Did she want to read the letter? Or was she putting that off right along with finishing the journal?

Why can't I finish what I started here? Why am I stalling?

But before she could lift the aged seal, she heard a knock at the front door. Rory. Always prompt. And yet he was early tonight. A good excuse to stall out again.

Should she ask him to sit with her while she read this?

No. Her mother had left it for her eyes only. It would have to wait a little bit longer.

Glancing longingly at the yellowed envelope, Vanessa took a deep breath and opened the front door. When she saw Rory, she had to take another breath.

Dressed in a crisp light blue shirt and pressed khakis along with polished brown loafers, he looked good. So good that Vanessa wanted to reach out and smooth his always this-side-of-disheveled, dark-blond bangs.

Instead, she enjoyed the way his eyes moved over her.

"You look like a movie star wrapped up in a summer package. A summer movie. A blockbuster."

She couldn't stop the giggle that bubbled up in her throat. "I've never had quite that kind of compliment before."

"And I rarely wear real shoes on a date," he said as he came inside and kicked the door shut. "We could be in a fifties sitcom."

"And yet here we stand in real life."

"I like real life better," he replied as he tugged her into his arms and danced her around. Then he leaned down and gave her a gentle kiss. "And we have plenty of room in here now."

"Yes." She pulled back and swung her arms wide. "We did it, Rory."

"You did it," he replied, pride in his eyes. "You did it and now, this place looks like a different house."

She smiled at that. "I tried to leave a few pieces to showcase the Craftsman features. And the spaciousness of this place. I'd forgotten how beautiful this house used to be."

Rory tucked a finger underneath her chin. "How ya doing?"

"I'm good. Okay. Sad but happy, too. I feel as if I've cleaned out a lot of the clutter in my mind, too." She almost told him about the envelope but held off.

He checked his watch. "We have a lot to talk about, don't we?"

"Yes. Let me grab my purse." She hurried to the desk and picked up the straw clutch she'd found to finish her outfit, her gaze drifting over the journal and the letter.

She wanted this special time with Rory. Later tonight, she'd finally sit down and take care of this one last task.

Reading the rest of the intimate details of her mother's strange, sometimes happy, sometimes sad, life.

* * *

The quaint French restaurant sat on the pass where the lake followed a tributary out into the big bay. Rory had asked for a table out on the patio, overlooking the water. A perfect spot for one of the Gulf's famous sunsets.

The night was perfect. A gentle tropical breeze teased at Vanessa's hair while he longed to take every pin and clip out of it and pull his fingers through it. Seagulls lifted out over the water, their soft caws as much a part of his life as praying. Candles and flowers adorned the white tablecloth, and an attentive waiter refilled their drinks and water without either of them having to lift a finger.

"This place is so beautiful, Rory," Vanessa said, her smile lighting up the gloaming. "I can't believe we're on a real date."

"Our first real date. My first date with anyone since…"

"Since you lost your wife," she finished. "Do you still miss her?"

"All the time," he admitted. "But I'm all about waiting on God's timing. Or at least I was until I met you."

Vanessa's eyes grew misty. "Are you sure? I mean, you two were so in love. This has to be hard."

"Hey, I'm okay. I'll be all right." He reached for her hand. "I had this battle going on in my head. I couldn't let go, but I think Allison would approve of you."

"Good to know." She took a sip of her drink. "I've dated so many men but nothing special, obviously."

"Does that include me?"

She gave him an indulgent smile that made his throat go dry. "You know you're very special. You've been so much more to me than someone to date. You've counseled me, consoled me, taught me grace and forgiveness and…made me rethink my whole way of life, including my future."

His heart hammered like a swinging pendulum. "Hey, I'm good, what can I say?"

"You are good. A good man."

He reached for her hand. "And since I'm so good, are you considering a future closer to me? As in, across the street? Or even closer?"

Her eyes went dark. "I'm considering a lot of things. But I don't know if I can live in that house again."

"You know, fresh paint and new furniture can—"

"Cover a multitude of sins?"

"Can give you a new perspective," he said, wishing he could wipe away the stains that only she could see.

"I'll have to think about keeping the house," she said.

Rory wisely changed the subject. They talked about the weather, about Blain and Rikki's wedding on Sunday, about her business and how much she loved finding and reselling wonderful collectibles. He told her about some of the fishing trips he'd been on with his buddies and about some of his darkest days during his deployment.

By the time their entrées had come—chicken for her and seafood for him—they were laughing and enjoying each other. All of the issues holding them apart seemed to settle down with the setting sun.

He held her hand while they waited for dessert, and together, they watched the bright golden sun slipping behind the water, its light leaving the heavens and the water washed in muted pinks and bronzed yellows. Cameras snapped the moment all around them, but Rory and Vanessa sat silent and held this moment close. That intimacy lasted through the crème brûlée and coffee, too.

And Rory knew in his heart, this was the woman for him.

Then he prayed that somehow Vanessa felt the same.

He kissed her good-night. Over and over. While they stood on the porch.

Vanessa finally slapped at his shirt. "Miss Fanny will be scandalized if you don't stop."

"Miss Fanny is a forward-thinking romantic who will appreciate that I've finally found a woman who can meet my high standards and amazingly handsome looks."

"You are so cute."

"Yes, I am that, too, of course."

He kissed her before she could form a retort. Then he whispered, "But you are beautiful and talented and you smell like spring and you're way out of my range, darlin'. I'm amazed you even looked at me twice."

"I tried not to," she reminded him. "Now I can't stop looking at you."

"I like looking at you while you're looking at me."

Vanessa didn't want to move out of his arms, but she was tired. Happy but exhausted. "I have to go inside before dawn, Rory."

"Hmmmm. We could cuddle in the swing all night."

"The mosquitoes will like that."

"I'll nibble on your neck and keep them away."

"Scandalous."

And tempting.

She pushed away and grinned at him. "You have a busy day tomorrow, too. Cleaning up the church, then rehearsal dinner for Blain and Rikki and then your sermon Sunday and then the wedding."

"I'll see you at the wedding. And in church, too."

"I plan to be at both. And I can help with cleanup tomorrow. We want the church to look good for that wedding."

He finally let out a sigh and stepped backward. "If I don't leave now, I'll never want to leave." But he took her hand in his and held it, their arms stretched out like a connecting bridge. "I want you to think long and hard about this, Vanessa. About how much you'll miss me if you leave."

"I know I'll miss you."

"And you know I'll miss you, too, don't you?"

"I believe that, yes."

"Okay then. We've established a strong attraction and we have to figure out what to do about it. But later, darling."

"Later," she said. "I enjoyed dinner."

"Me, too." He waved good-night, and then she watched him, heard him whistling and smiled to herself.

She didn't want to leave him. She was in love with Rory.

Somehow, she'd figure out a way to tell him that... and deal with it.

Chapter Twenty-One

An hour later, Vanessa settled on the couch with her mother's journal and the envelope she'd been avoiding all day. She realized avoidance was her specialty. She'd avoided facing the truth in her life and she'd avoided any serious relationships. She'd avoided coming back to confront her mother about the things they'd left unsaid through the years. She'd avoided making sure the world knew about Gregory Pardue and what he'd done to her. And in a weird way, selling vintage clothes and collectibles had allowed her to avoid moving into the future.

She'd also avoided God and the kind of love that only having faith could bring into her life.

But she had to face facts now. No more excuses. She was done clinging to the past.

And because she wanted Rory in her life and that might mean moving back to Millbrook, she knew it was now or never on getting through this journal.

But first, the envelope, please.

She opened it and found a one-page letter from her mother.

And a birth certificate.

By the time she'd finished reading the letter and glancing over the birth certificate, Vanessa's whole life had flashed through her mind with a glaring intensity that left her gasping for breath, her sobs caught in her throat.

She didn't have to read her mother's journal to realize her whole life had been based on a lie.

Rory shoved another box of clothing into the big rental truck they'd loaded with what was left from the rummage sale.

"This should be the last of it," Alec called out, sweat beading on his forehead as he shoved another box up the loading ramp.

Rory nodded and glanced across the street. Vanessa had never shown up to help, and her car had been gone when he'd gotten up. Early-morning errands?

He'd get a shower and go over once he'd checked on the gathering hall. But Wanda and a few other volunteers were giving it a once-over with the vacuum and brooms. The place would be spotless before Wanda released her crew.

Kandi lifted up a bag full of jewelry to him. "Have you seen Vanessa? She called Miss Wanda yesterday after we left the sale and said she had some things for me."

Rory shook his head. "No. I'll call her later. Her car's not in the driveway. Must have gone out early for something."

"I know where she is."

Both Rory and Kandi turned to find Miss Fanny standing there leaning on her walker, a gloomy expression on her face.

"Where?" Rory asked, concern mounting only because Miss Fanny had never looked so glum.

Miss Fanny waited until he finished with the truck and came down the ramp. "She's gone, Rory."

"Gone?" He checked the house again. "What do you mean?"

"I found this tucked into my screen door." Miss Fanny handed him a square blue envelope. "It has your name on it."

Kandi eyed the envelope and then shook her head. "She told me she might not be around for long. But I thought—"

"Me, too," Miss Fanny said. "I thought we'd won her over."

Kandi shot both of them a disgusted stare. "I should know not to count on anybody or anything."

"Hey, we haven't heard what happened," Rory warned, his heart sinking. "I'll read this, and then maybe I'll call her."

"Right." Kandi turned and stalked back into the church.

"I'll leave you to it," Miss Fanny said to Rory, her eyes full of sympathy. "I hope it's nothing bad."

Rory hoped the same. "I'll find out, good or bad."

After they'd finished and he'd closed up the church, he went up to the little porch of his garage apartment and sat down in the rickety old lawn chair. Then he opened the card.

Rory,
I have some urgent business in Alabama. I don't know when I'll be back. Thank you again for last night. And for everything.
Vanessa

That was it. No explanation, no reason for leaving in

the middle of the night. Or at least before dawn, since he'd been up that long. Rory pulled out his phone. Not even a text or missed call. It was close to two in the afternoon. He had a few hours before the rehearsal dinner for the Kent-Alvanetti wedding.

Taking out his phone, he called Vanessa.

No answer. It went straight to voice mail.

Now he was really worried.

After finding the number on her website, he called Vanessa's Vintage boutique in New Orleans. But the sales associate who answered said they hadn't heard from Vanessa today.

"She told us she'd call when she was on her way back," the woman said. "But for now, that's probably going to be late next week since she's mostly finished with clearing out her mother's house."

Rory thanked the woman and ended the call.

"Hey!"

He glanced down to find Alec standing by the steps up to his place. "Everything okay?"

Rory nodded and hurried down the steps. "Vanessa is gone. Left me a note saying she had to go to Alabama."

Alec rubbed the scar that slashed across one cheek. "Well, she does have property there now. Maybe something came up."

"Maybe," Rory said. "But she could have called. I'm worried. Leaving a note seems odd, considering."

Considering how they'd left things last night.

"How was she last time you saw her?"

"She was great. We had a good time. I thought things were looking up."

Alec slapped his hand against Rory's arm. "I'm sure she's still dealing with a lot, so try not to worry. Maybe she'll be back later today."

Rory hoped so, too. And he prayed all day long, about a lot of things. When he still hadn't heard from her later that night after the rehearsal dinner, he had to accept that she might have left because she was scared of what they felt for each other.

That meant he'd have to give her some time to decide what she really wanted to do. Or if she really wanted to be with him after all.

Vanessa stood looking up at the staircase of the Tudor-style house in Birmingham that had belonged to Richard Tucker.

Her house now. But not just because the man was generous.

She was his daughter.

A mirror centered on the wall in the entryway caught her eye. Vanessa studied herself, seeing it all so clearly now.

Richard Tucker was her father.

The dark-haired man who'd come to visit when she was young.

The man who'd bought the house in Millbrook Lake for her mother, even when he was married to another woman.

A woman who couldn't have children.

The man who'd made her mother cry over and over again.

His wife had died and Richard had come back to Cora at long last, after years of quick visits and whispered words. But neither of her parents had thought it important to explain this to Vanessa.

We felt it best to leave things as they were. We were happy and we tried to make you happy. It could

have made things worse, telling you the truth since
Richard had been absent from our lives for so long.
I hope you will forgive us. We both loved you so
much. I tried to tell you so many times.

Her mother's words in the letter.

She'd read the journal, too, even though it had made
her sick to her stomach and boiling mad with anger.

But the last words of her mother's journal had finally
saved Vanessa by showing her the final thread to the past.

*One day, your father's legacy will become yours. He
worked very hard to make sure you'd have a secure future. Vanessa, please don't waste this opportunity. Use
this gift to move forward with your life. And learn from
our mistakes.*

Always be honest.

Always be kind.

Trust in God.

Fall in love.

Vanessa wondered why none of this had been mentioned in the will, but then Cora was ever the dramatic
one. Her mother knew she'd find the journal. Knew she'd
be curious.

So Cora had created one last piece of art. Pictures and
words, pasted like a collage of Vanessa's life, against
paper, with glue that would stick for a lifetime. Cora
also knew that if anyone else found the journal or the
letter, they'd make sure Vanessa got them. But mostly,
her mother knew that Vanessa would come back to the
house because Vanessa loved old things. Because Vanessa would want to know about the past.

So here she stood, in a house that could have been
her home. Vanessa moved around the sprawling, elegant

mansion, her mind thinking of so many scenarios. Should she sell this place?

Move here and try to recapture her youth?

Go home to Rory?

She voted for the last one.

Checking her watch, she saw the late hour.

Then she pulled out her phone.

Rory picked up on the fourth ring. "Hello?"

His voice slid over her in a husky whisper.

"It's me," she said, forcing the tears out of her words.

"Hi. Are you okay?"

"I am now. I wanted you to know… I'm coming home."

"Home? As in, to me?"

"Home to you, yes."

"When?"

"I don't know. Maybe soon. Maybe in a few days. Or weeks."

"Vanessa—"

"I'll explain everything when I get there."

"Are you sure you're all right?"

"Not yet. But I will be as soon as I see you again."

"Vanessa, I—"

"Don't. Not yet. I'll see you soon, Rory."

"Okay, but when you get here will you please stop interrupting me?"

"Probably not. I have to go."

She stood in the big, empty house and realized big houses didn't make homes and bad memories didn't have to ruin a house or a home. Or a future full of promise.

When her phone rang again, she shook her head. "Rory…"

But it wasn't Rory.

"Why did you leave? You know Rory loves you."

Kandi.

"It's hard to explain."

"Complicated? Right. Look, I know all about complicated. You're gonna have to do better than that."

"It's tough. I found out something that kind of rocked my world."

"In a good way?"

"Good and bad. I'm still in shock."

"Well, snap out of it. We… I mean… Rory needs you."

"I'm coming back," Vanessa said to reassure Kandi and herself. "And once I get back there, I don't think I'm ever going to leave again."

"That's more like it. Later."

"Later."

Vanessa put away her phone, her mind still on Kandi. She couldn't disappoint the girl. She didn't want to disappoint Rory either. Mostly, she didn't want to let go of the good parts of Millbrook Lake. The church and her friends and Rory.

I can't avoid this. I love him. I want to be with him.

Help me, Lord. Show me the courage to follow my heart instead of holding on to my pain.

She went from room to room in the big house, studied the huge, airy bedrooms and several roomy bathrooms, stood in the huge kitchen and imagined many happy times here, sat on a white wicker chair in the second-floor solarium and thought about reading books and drinking tea right here, and by the time she'd made it back downstairs, she knew what she wanted to do with this house.

And she knew she wasn't going to sell the Millbrook Lake house.

"I don't think she's coming back," Rory told Alec and Blain right before the wedding was about to begin.

"Something caused her to run. Something about that house and her mother. Maybe she finally read the rest of that clunky journal she kept moving from room to room."

Blain quirked his detective eyebrows up in a question. "Do you think she found out something in the journal? Or that she's using any excuse to avoid commitment?"

"Sounds like the voice of experience," Alec said with a wink toward Blain.

"It is the voice of experience," Blain replied. "I wasn't one for committing to a relationship until I met Rikki."

"The least likely candidate," Alec said.

"Same with Vanessa," Rory said, nodding. "She made it clear she didn't want marriage and children. And she knows how I feel about that."

"Maybe she just wants a low-key relationship with no strings attached," Blain said.

Rory could hear the organ music starting up. People were piling into the church. The smell of fresh lilies and sprays of jasmine filled the air. He had to get it together for Blain's sake. And the fact that Rikki would throttle him if he didn't present a happy face while he read their vows to them.

"I could live with that," he told Blain. "For a while."

Alec adjusted his tie. "Yes, but you want more, right?"

Rory nodded. "I fought against wanting more for a long time. After I lost Allison—"

"You deserve more," Blain said. "And Preacher, you might take some of your own advice and trust in the man upstairs."

Rory couldn't argue with that. "You're right. And it's time to get you to the altar. Your bride will come looking if we're late."

Blain grinned, his dark eyes bright with love. "I can't believe I'm getting married today."

"We're both happy for you," Alec said. "I love being a married man."

Rory would love that, too. But while he was happy for his two lovestruck friends, he had to wonder if he'd ever have that dream of marriage and a family again.

Vanessa might talk herself right out of coming back to Millbrook Lake.

She stood in the back of the church until she saw an open spot in the very last pew. Vanessa slid in without being noticed and took in the scene.

White lilies and baby's breath, trailing sprays of jasmine mixed with tiny white and pink roses. Candlelight and soft music. Blain looked so happy, so expectant, waiting for his bride.

Rory stood staring up the aisle, his own expression expectant. Had he seen her come in? She'd driven across Alabama to get here, but it had taken her a lifetime to find him.

The music swelled and Rikki came into view, her proud father, Franco Alvanetti, walking her down the aisle. She looked beautiful in the slinky white dress that flowed out into a long train complete with a huge bow tied at the back.

Vanessa watched, her eyes tearing up, as Rikki and Blain said their vows. Rory officiated with pride and humor, making everyone laugh and cry.

"Cherish this moment," he told the couple. "Cherish the people you love. And keep God in the center of your lives."

He said a prayer, and then he told Blain to kiss his bride.

After that, they turned around and he presented them to the guests as man and wife.

Man and wife.

Soon, everyone poured out of the church to head out to the swank Alvanetti estate. But Vanessa held back and walked up to the altar and closed her eyes. She needed a minute. Just a minute. To tell God that she was home now.

When she opened her eyes and turned to leave, she saw him.

Rory. Standing at the back of the church in a nice navy suit. He looked lovable and scruffy, like a lost puppy come home. Like a man who'd been searching for someone for a long time, his blue eyes bright with hope and surprise.

Vanessa hurried toward him. They met somewhere in the middle of the long aisle.

"You're here. Now." He looked completely surprised.

"I told you I'd be back."

"But—"

Panic rushed over her. "Are you glad I'm back?"

He reached out his hands to hers and laced their fingers together. "I'm thrilled that you're back. I thought it might take you a while."

"I thought about taking a while," she admitted. "You know, avoiding what I could see so clearly."

He gave her one of his soft smiles. "And what do you see so clearly now?"

She didn't want to cry, but she couldn't stop the tears. "You. And that dream. Remember when I told you about standing in the garden at Caldwell House, how I wanted that one day—the garden, the house, the sound of children laughing."

His eyes got misty, too. "I remember."

"I think I've found it, Rory. And when I turned around just now and saw you, I felt it, too. That feeling you told me I'd feel one day. It's like a warmth flowing through me and over me, and my soul is full of lightness and joy."

"Yeah, that feeling," he said, pulling her close.

Vanessa held him there, silent tears moving down her face. "Richard Tucker was my real father."

Rory lifted away. "What?"

"She left me a letter and my birth certificate. He was married, but they fell in love and had an ongoing affair. He and his wife never had children and then his wife died. He bought my mother the house here. And of course, he came here and married her, but they both felt it would be too confusing to tell me the truth. So as a conciliation prize, he left everything to me. Everything, except the truth."

"Vanessa, I'm so sorry," Rory said on a shattered whisper. "I don't know what to say. Are you sure you can handle this?"

"I didn't think so at first. I got in the car last night and left, determined to go to Birmingham and walk through the other house. I think I was searching for something, a sign maybe."

"And what did you find?"

"A sad, empty house. But I also found closure because now I know the truth." She wiped her eyes and smiled up at him. "And I realized that instead of avoiding the truth, I wanted to be here with you—living our truth."

Rory couldn't believe what Vanessa had told him. "What will you do now?"

She took his hand, and they started toward the back of the church. "Well, our friends are about to celebrate their wedding day, so first, I want to have a big piece of wedding cake."

He grinned at that. "We can make that happen. They're probably wondering what happened to me after the photo session was done. I came back in to lock things up."

"Then we'd better hurry," she said. "We'll take my car."

When they reached her driveway, Rory stared over at the house. "Are you still going to sell this place?"

"No." She gave him a hopeful smile. "I'm going to renovate it. Sweep it clean of all the cobwebs and secrets. I want it light and bright and sunny and warm."

His heart did a little flip of joy. Before she could get in the car, he tugged her close. Her eyes were clear and sure, no cobwebs or secrets left there. She looked young and carefree and …at peace. "It's a really big house, Vanessa. You don't need to be there all alone."

"I won't be alone." She reached up to kiss him. "You'll be nearby."

"No. I don't like that," he said. "I want to live there with you. I want to marry you."

"Yes," she said.

"Yes?" He laughed, glad she agreed. "Did you just interrupt me again?"

"I didn't interrupt you."

"Can I at least ask the question?"

"Yes. Yes."

"Okay." He wanted to laugh and cry, but he held his emotions back and took her hands in his. "Will you marry me, Vanessa?"

"Yes."

"Are you willing to have my children?"

"Yes."

"Are you mad that I don't have a ring for you yet?"

"No. But I can get you a good deal on one through Vanessa's Vintage."

"I love you," he said.

"I love you." She kissed him again, and then they got in the little car. When she put the top down, they laughed into the wind and made plans for the future.

"I'm going to turn the Birmingham house into a girls' home," she told him. "And I want to help Kandi with college and maybe give her a job."

"And I want to remodel the Craftsman and make it so beautiful, you'll only have happy memories there," he told her.

By the time they reached the reception, they'd made a lifetime of plans. A commitment to be together for a long, long time.

Rory got out and came around to open her door. "Let's go party."

Vanessa laughed as he lifted her up in his arms and swung her around. "I love you so much," he told her.

Then they heard a grunt off by the big garage. Hunter Lawson sat there on his motorcycle, watching them. "And another one bites the dust."

But he was smiling, a twist of bittersweet mixed with the happiness in his eyes.

"Thanks," Rory said. "You can be my best man."

"Ain't gonna happen," Hunter said. Then he cranked his bike and left.

"He never stays at parties for very long," Rory explained. "But I love me a good party."

They laughed and held hands as they headed through the house. They found everyone in the backyard by the pool, enjoying the beautiful view, where the lake and the big bay merged.

"There you are," Blain called out with a grin.
"Better late than never," Rory replied.
And he felt sure God thought that a lot, too.

* * * * *

Dear Reader:

I have to admit this story captured my heart. I fell for Rory the moment he came into my head. He had a good soul, and he cared about other people. He needed a special woman in his life after all the things he'd been through. In spite of his pain, he became a true man of God.

Vanessa was the opposite. Bitter and disillusioned, hurting and skeptical. What better person to show her that life can still be full of joy? Rory didn't even realize that he needed someone to take care of him, too. Sometimes, we work so hard to help others, we forget to take care of nurturing our own souls.

I hope you enjoyed Rory and Vanessa's story. Please visit me through my website at www.lenoraworth.com. And I hope you'll look for Hunter's story as my Men of Millbrook Lake series continues. I might not ever leave Millbrook Lake.

Until next time, may the angels watch over you. Always.

Lenora Worth

REQUEST YOUR FREE BOOKS!

2 FREE INSPIRATIONAL NOVELS

PLUS 2
FREE
MYSTERY GIFTS

Love Inspired®

YES! Please send me 2 FREE Love Inspired® novels and my 2 FREE mystery gifts (gifts are worth about $10). After receiving them, if I don't wish to receive any more books, I can return the shipping statement marked "cancel." If I don't cancel, I will receive 6 brand-new novels every month and be billed just $4.99 per book in the U.S. or $5.49 per book in Canada. That's a saving of at least 17% off the cover price. It's quite a bargain! Shipping and handling is just 50¢ per book in the U.S. and 75¢ per book in Canada.* I understand that accepting the 2 free books and gifts places me under no obligation to buy anything. I can always return a shipment and cancel at any time. Even if I never buy another book, the two free books and gifts are mine to keep forever.

105/305 IDN GH5P

Name _____ (PLEASE PRINT)

Address _____ Apt. #

City _____ State/Prov. _____ Zip/Postal Code

Signature (if under 18, a parent or guardian must sign)

Mail to the **Reader Service:**
IN U.S.A.: P.O. Box 1867, Buffalo, NY 14240-1867
IN CANADA: P.O. Box 609, Fort Erie, Ontario L2A 5X3

Are you a subscriber to Love Inspired® books
and want to receive the larger-print edition?
Call 1-800-873-8635 or visit www.ReaderService.com.

* Terms and prices subject to change without notice. Prices do not include applicable taxes. Sales tax applicable in N.Y. Canadian residents will be charged applicable taxes. Offer not valid in Quebec. This offer is limited to one order per household. Not valid for current subscribers to Love Inspired books. All orders subject to credit approval. Credit or debit balances in a customer's account(s) may be offset by any other outstanding balance owed by or to the customer. Please allow 4 to 6 weeks for delivery. Offer available while quantities last.

Your Privacy—The Reader Service is committed to protecting your privacy. Our Privacy Policy is available online at www.ReaderService.com or upon request from the Reader Service.

We make a portion of our mailing list available to reputable third parties that offer products we believe may interest you. If you prefer that we not exchange your name with third parties, or if you wish to clarify or modify your communication preferences, please visit us at www.ReaderService.com/consumerschoice or write to us at Reader Service Preference Service, P.O. Box 9062, Buffalo, NY 14240-9062. Include your complete name and address.

LI15

"So you didn't like it here?" Vic asked. "Coming every
summer?"

"I missed my friends back home, but there were parts
I liked."

"I remember seeing you girls in church on Sunday."

"Part of the deal," Lauren said, a faint smile teasing her
mouth. "And I didn't mind that part, either. The message
was always good, once I started really listening. I can't
remember who the pastor was, but what he said resonated
with me."

"Jodie and Erin would attend some of the youth events,
didn't they?"

"Erin more than any of us."

"I remember my brother Dean talking about her," Vic
said. "I think he had a secret crush on her."

"He was impetuous, wasn't he?"

"That's being kind. But he's settled now."

Thoughts of Dean brought up the same problem that
had brought him to the ranch.

His deal with Lauren's father.

"So, I hate to be a broken record," he continued, "but

I was wondering if I could come by the house tomorrow. To go through your father's papers."

Lauren sighed.

Vic tamped down his immediate apology. He had nothing to feel bad about. He was just looking out for his brother's interests.

"Yes. Of course. Though—" She stopped herself there. "Sorry. You probably know better what you're looking for."

Vic shot her a glance across the cab of the truck. "I'm not trying to jeopardize your deal. When I first leased the ranch from your father, it was so that my brother could have his own place. And I'm hoping to protect that promise I made him. Especially now. After his accident."

"I understand," Lauren said, her smile apologetic. "I know what it's like to protect siblings."

"Are you the oldest?"

"Erin and I are twins, but I'm older by twenty minutes."

Lauren smiled at him. And as their eyes held, he felt it again. An unexpected rush of attraction. When her eyes grew ever so slightly wider, he wondered if she felt it, too.

He dragged his attention back to the road.

You're no judge of your feelings, he reminded himself, his hands tightening on the steering wheel as if reining in his attraction to this enigmatic woman.

He'd made mistakes in the past, falling for the wrong person. He couldn't do it again. He couldn't afford to.

Especially not with Lauren.

Don't miss
TRUSTING THE COWBOY
by Carolyne Aarsen, available July 2016 wherever
Love Inspired® books and ebooks are sold.

www.LoveInspired.com

LIEXP0616

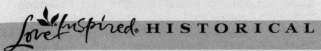
At last, CJ thought. Help was on the way.

With each step Molly took in his direction, he felt the tension draining out of him. She was a calming influence and the stability they all needed—not just Sarah and Anna, but CJ, too.

If she ever left him…

Not the point, he told himself.

She looked uncommonly beautiful this morning in a blue cotton dress with a white lace collar and long sleeves. The cut of the garment emphasized her tiny waist and petite frame.

He attempted to swallow past the lump in his throat without much success. Molly took his breath away.

If he were from a different family…

"Miss Molly," Anna called out. "Miss Molly, over here! We're over here."

Sarah wasn't content with merely waving. She pulled her hand free of CJ's and raced to meet Molly across the small expanse of grass. Anna followed hard on her sister's heels.

Molly greeted both girls with a hug and a kiss on the top of their heads.

"Well, look who it is." She stepped back and smiled down

at the twins. "My two favorite girls in all of Little Horn, Texas. And don't you look especially pretty this morning."

"Unca Corny picked out our dresses," Sarah told her.

"He tried to make breakfast." Anna swayed her shoulders back and forth with little-girl pride. "He didn't do so good. He burned the oatmeal and Cookie had to make more."

Molly's compassionate gaze met his. "Sounds like you had an…interesting morning."

CJ chuckled softly. "Though I wouldn't want to repeat the experience anytime soon, we survived well enough."

"Miss Molly, look. I'm wearing my favorite pink ribbon." Sarah touched the floppy bow with reverent fingers. "I tied it all by myself."

"You did a lovely job." Under the guise of inspecting the ribbon, Molly retied the bow, then moved it around until it sat straight on the child's head. "Pink is my favorite color."

"It's Pa's favorite, too." Sarah's gaze skittered toward the crowded tent. "I wore it just for him."

The wistful note in her voice broke CJ's heart. He shared a tortured look with Molly.

Her ragged sigh told him she was thinking along the same lines as he was. His brother always made it to church, a fact the twins had reminded him of this morning.

"Pa says Sunday is the most important day of the week," Sarah had told him, while Anna had added, "And we're never supposed to miss Sunday service. Not ever."

Somewhere along the way, the two had gotten it into their heads that Ned would show up at church today. CJ wasn't anywhere near as confident. If Ned didn't make an appearance, the twins would know that their father was truly gone.

Don't miss
STAND-IN RANCHER DADDY
by Renee Ryan, available July 2016 wherever
Love Inspired® Historical books and ebooks are sold.

www.LoveInspired.com